young justice ™

2

STONE ARCH BOOKS
a capstone imprint

STONE ARCH BOOKS™

Published in 2012
A Capstone Imprint
1710 Roe Crest Drive
North Mankato, MN 56003
www.capstonepub.com

Originally published by DC Comics in the U.S. in single
magazine form as Young Justice #2.
Copyright © 2012 DC Comics. All Rights Reserved.

DC Comics
1700 Broadway, New York, NY 10019
A Warner Bros. Entertainment Company

Printed in the United States of America
in Brainerd, Minnesota.
032012   006728ANGF12

Cataloging-in-Publication Data is available at the
Library of Congress website:
ISBN: 978-1-4342-4554-0 (library binding)

Summary: In this action-packed story, Superboy
discovers that an unwanted guest in the team's cave
is not really what he appears to be! Is the threat
deadly to only the Boy of Steel - or is the entire
Justice League in danger, as well?

STONE ARCH BOOKS

Ashley C. Andersen Zantop *Publisher*
Michael Dahl *Editorial Director*
Donald Lemke & Sean Tulien *Editors*
Heather Kindseth *Creative Director*
Brann Garvey *Designer*
Kathy McColley *Production Specialist*

DC COMICS

Scott Peterson & Jim Chadwick *Original U.S. Editors*
Michael McCalister *U.S. Assistant Editor*
Mike Norton *Cover Artist*

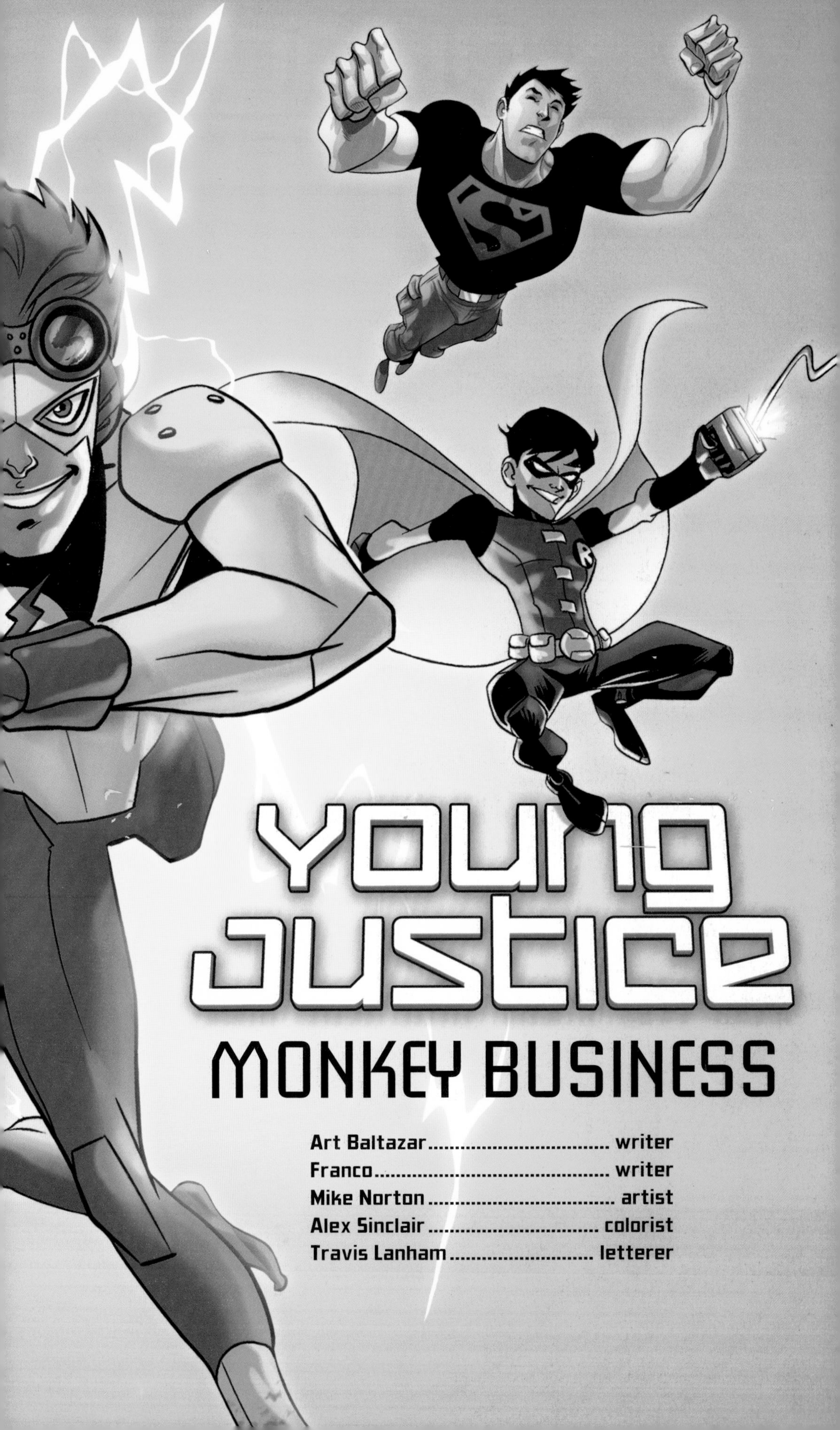

YOUNG JUSTICE

MONKEY BUSINESS

Art Baltazar .... writer
Franco .... writer
Mike Norton .... artist
Alex Sinclair .... colorist
Travis Lanham .... letterer

YOUNG JUSTICE™

AQUALAD

AGE: 16   **SECRET IDENTITY:** Kaldur' Ahm

BIO: Aquaman's apprentice; a cool, calm warrior and leader; totally amphibious with the ability to bend and shape water.

SUPERBOY

AGE: 16   **SECRET IDENTITY:** Conner Kent

BIO: Cloned from Superman; a shy and uncertain teenager; gifted with super-strength, infrared vision, and leaping abilities.

ARTEMIS

AGE: 15   **SECRET IDENTITY:** Classified

BIO: Green Arrow's niece; a dedicated and tough fighter; extremely talented in both archery and martial arts.

KID FLASH

AGE: 15   **SECRET IDENTITY:** Wally West

BIO: Partner of the Flash; a competitive team member, often lacking self-control; gifted with super-speed.

ROBIN

AGE: 13   **SECRET IDENTITY:** Dick Grayson

BIO: Partner of Batman; the youngest member of the team; talented acrobat, martial artist, and hacker.

MISS MARTIAN

AGE: 16   **SECRET IDENTITY:** M'gann M'orzz

BIO: Martian Manhunter's niece; polite and sweet; ability to shape-shift, read minds, transform, and fly.

THE STORY SO FAR...

Superboy and Miss Martian, members of the newly formed Young Justice team, explore the group's new headquarters. Unfortunately, they're not alone. The Joker is already inside - with a big surprise! Will the Clown Prince have the last laugh, or will Young Justice foil his plan...?

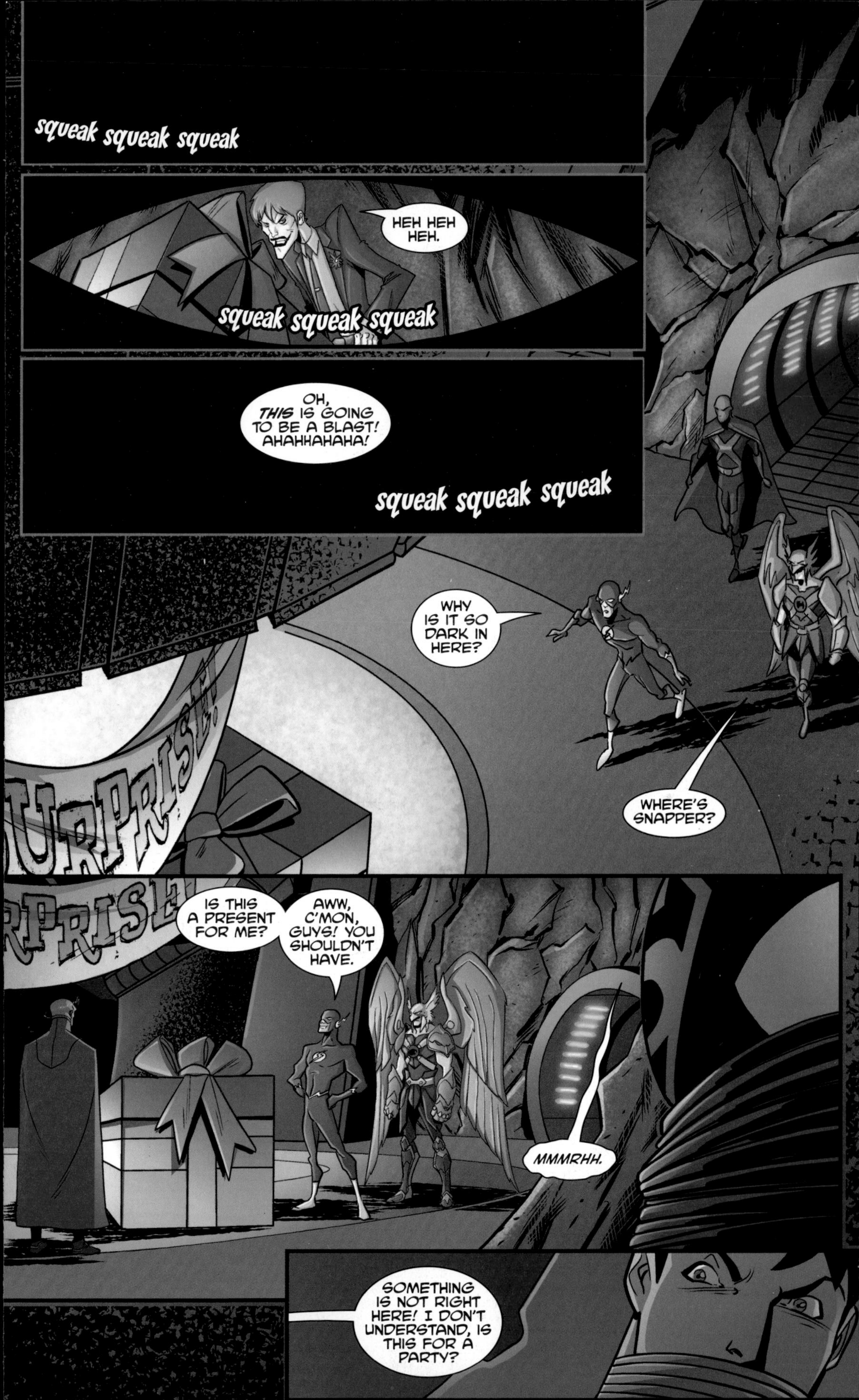
squeak squeak squeak
HEH HEH HEH.
squeak squeak squeak
OH, THIS IS GOING TO BE A BLAST! AHAHHAHAHA!
squeak squeak squeak
WHY IS IT SO DARK IN HERE?
WHERE'S SNAPPER?
SURPRISE!
IS THIS A PRESENT FOR ME?
AWW, C'MON, GUYS! YOU SHOULDN'T HAVE.
MMMRHH.
SOMETHING IS NOT RIGHT HERE! I DON'T UNDERSTAND, IS THIS FOR A PARTY?

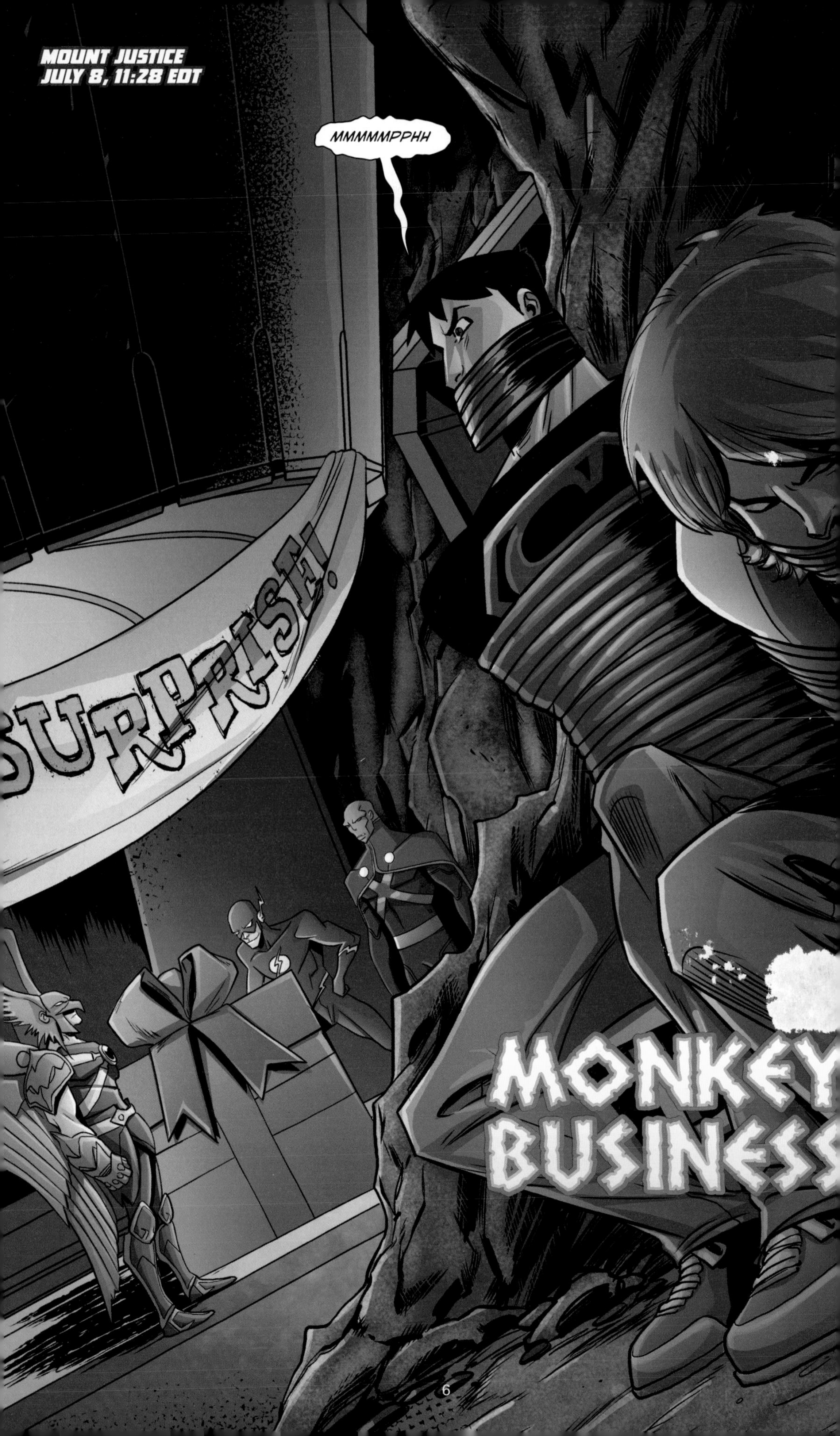
MOUNT JUSTICE
JULY 8, 11:28 EDT
MMMMMPPHH
SURPRISE!
MONKEY
BUSINESS

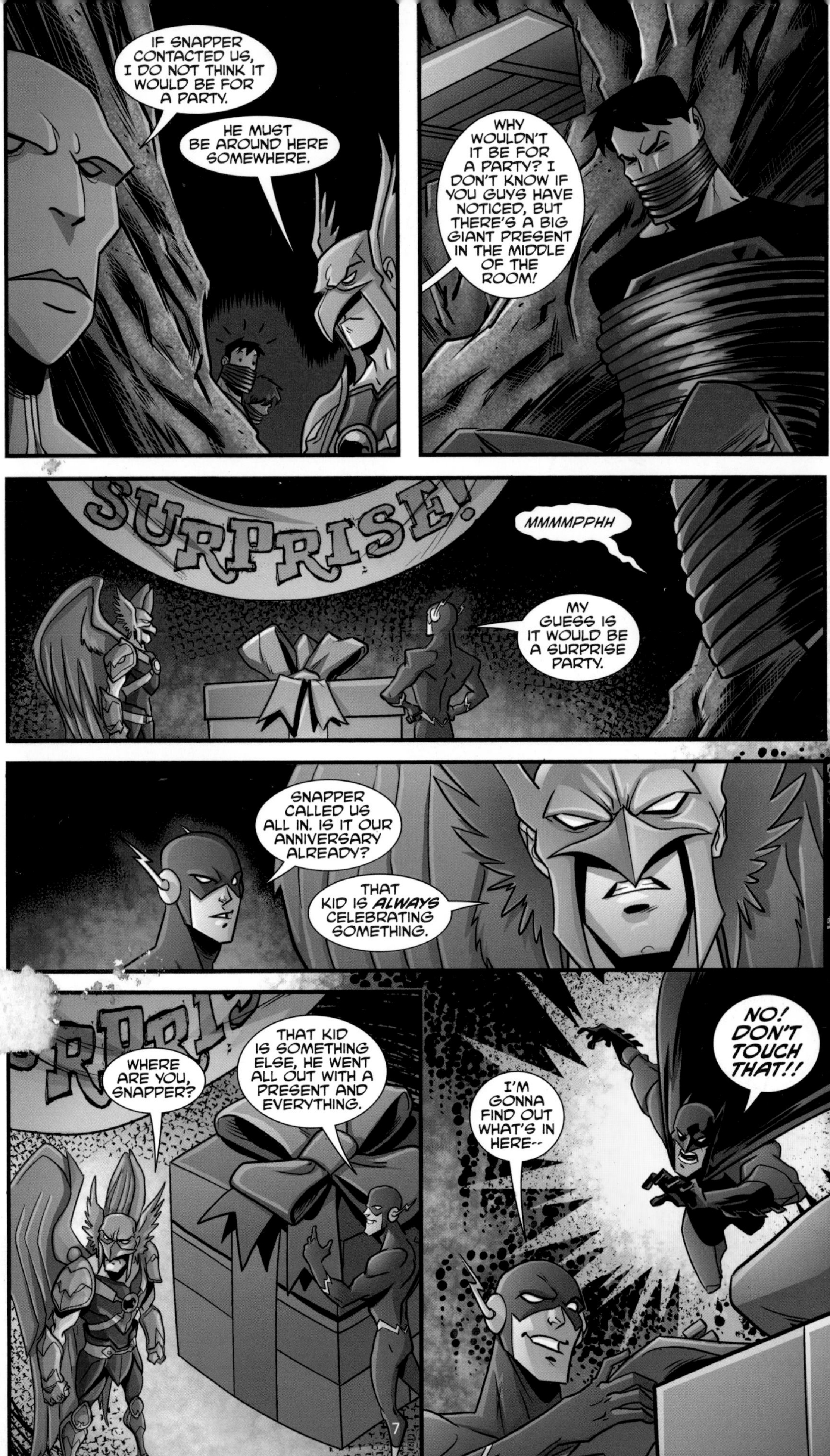
IF SNAPPER CONTACTED US, I DO NOT THINK IT WOULD BE FOR A PARTY.
HE MUST BE AROUND HERE SOMEWHERE.
WHY WOULDN'T IT BE FOR A PARTY? I DON'T KNOW IF YOU GUYS HAVE NOTICED, BUT THERE'S A BIG GIANT PRESENT IN THE MIDDLE OF THE ROOM!
SURPRISE!
MMMMPPHH
MY GUESS IS IT WOULD BE A SURPRISE PARTY.
SNAPPER CALLED US ALL IN. IS IT OUR ANNIVERSARY ALREADY?
THAT KID IS *ALWAYS* CELEBRATING SOMETHING.
WHERE ARE YOU, SNAPPER?
THAT KID IS SOMETHING ELSE, HE WENT ALL OUT WITH A PRESENT AND EVERYTHING.
I'M GONNA FIND OUT WHAT'S IN HERE--
NO! DON'T TOUCH THAT!!

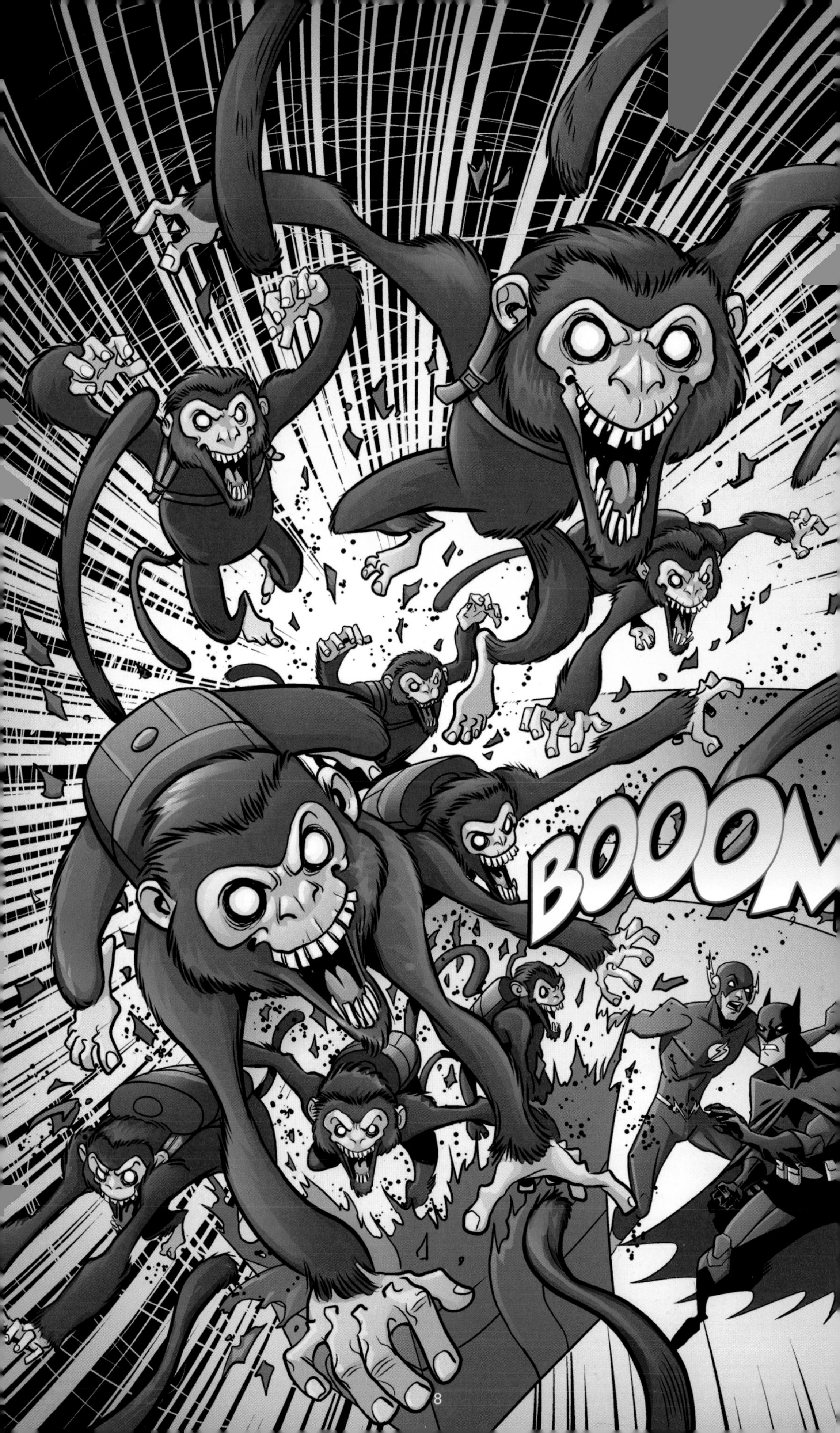
BOOOM

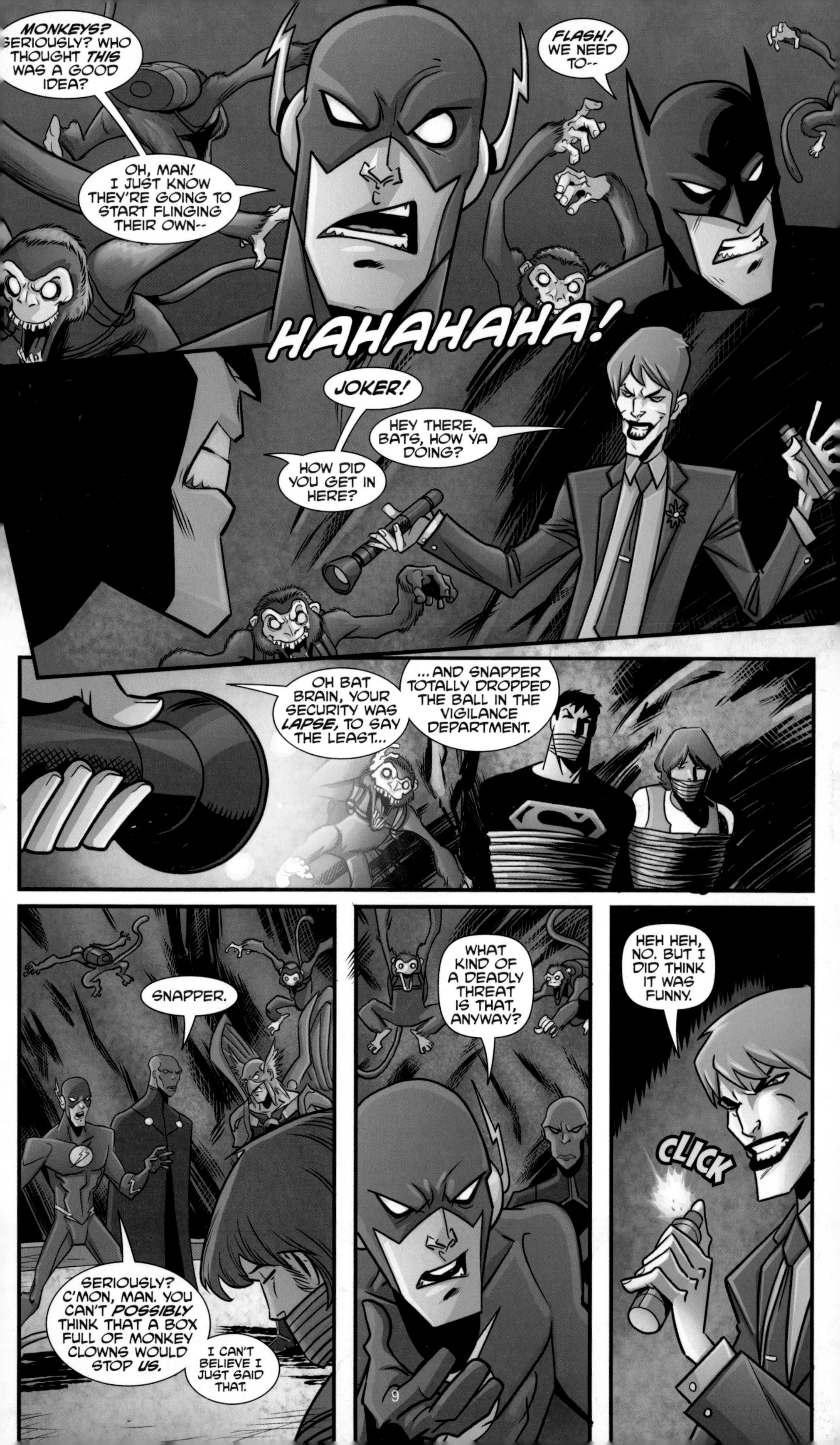
MONKEYS? SERIOUSLY? WHO THOUGHT THIS WAS A GOOD IDEA?
OH, MAN! I JUST KNOW THEY'RE GOING TO START FLINGING THEIR OWN--
FLASH! WE NEED TO--
HAHAHAHA!
JOKER!
HOW DID YOU GET IN HERE?
HEY THERE, BATS, HOW YA DOING?
OH BAT BRAIN, YOUR SECURITY WAS LAPSE, TO SAY THE LEAST...
...AND SNAPPER TOTALLY DROPPED THE BALL IN THE VIGILANCE DEPARTMENT.
SNAPPER.
SERIOUSLY? C'MON, MAN. YOU CAN'T POSSIBLY THINK THAT A BOX FULL OF MONKEY CLOWNS WOULD STOP US.
I CAN'T BELIEVE I JUST SAID THAT.
WHAT KIND OF A DEADLY THREAT IS THAT, ANYWAY?
HEH HEH, NO. BUT I DID THINK IT WAS FUNNY.
CLICK

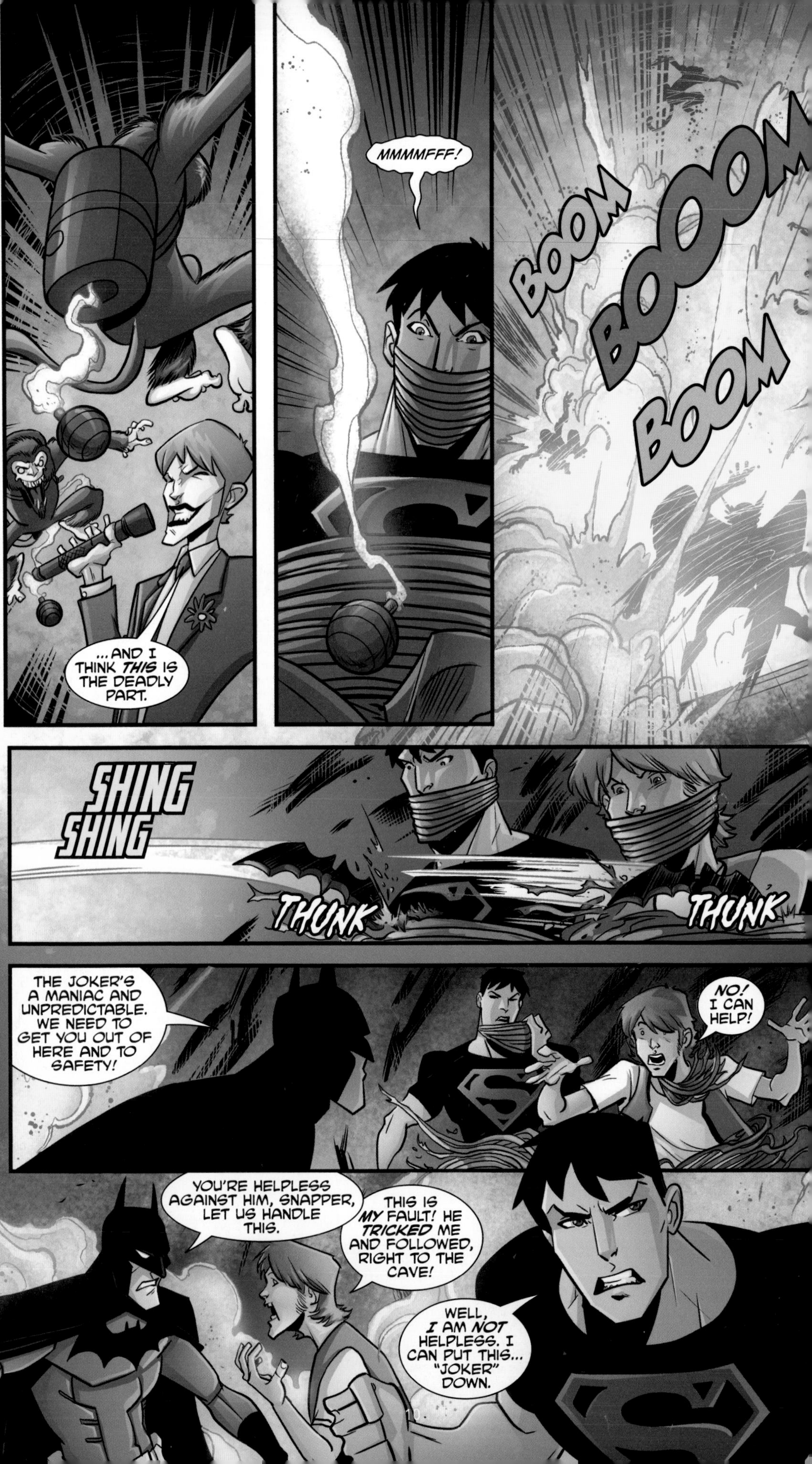
...AND I THINK THIS IS THE DEADLY PART.
MMMMFFF!
BOOM
BOOOOM
BOOM
SHING
SHING
THUNK
THUNK
THE JOKER'S A MANIAC AND UNPREDICTABLE. WE NEED TO GET YOU OUT OF HERE AND TO SAFETY!
NO! I CAN HELP!
YOU'RE HELPLESS AGAINST HIM, SNAPPER, LET US HANDLE THIS.
THIS IS MY FAULT! HE TRICKED ME AND FOLLOWED, RIGHT TO THE CAVE!
WELL, I AM NOT HELPLESS. I CAN PUT THIS... "JOKER" DOWN.

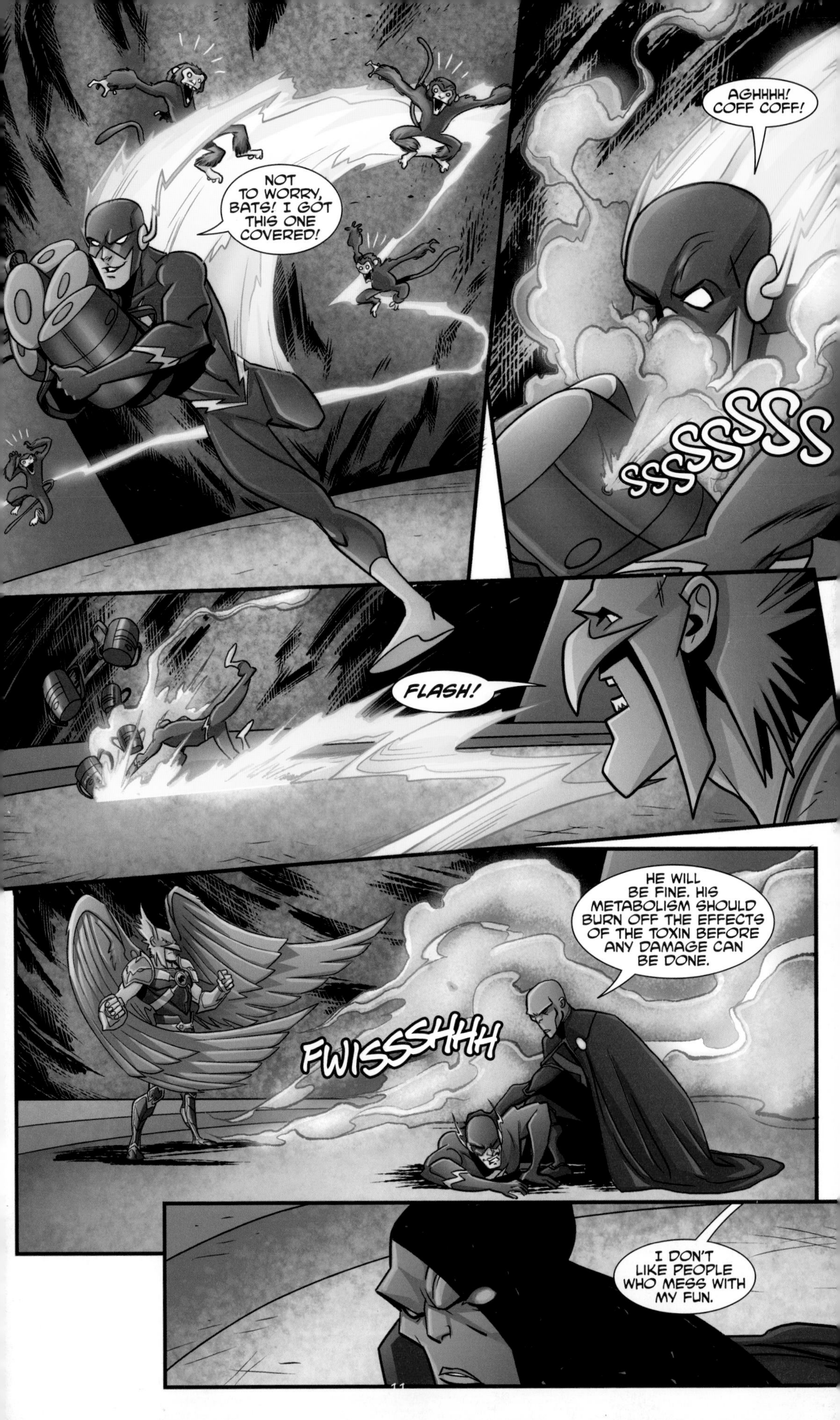
NOT TO WORRY, BATS! I GOT THIS ONE COVERED!
AGHHHH! COFF COFF!
SSSSSSSSS
FLASH!
HE WILL BE FINE. HIS METABOLISM SHOULD BURN OFF THE EFFECTS OF THE TOXIN BEFORE ANY DAMAGE CAN BE DONE.
FWISSSHHH
I DON'T LIKE PEOPLE WHO MESS WITH MY FUN.

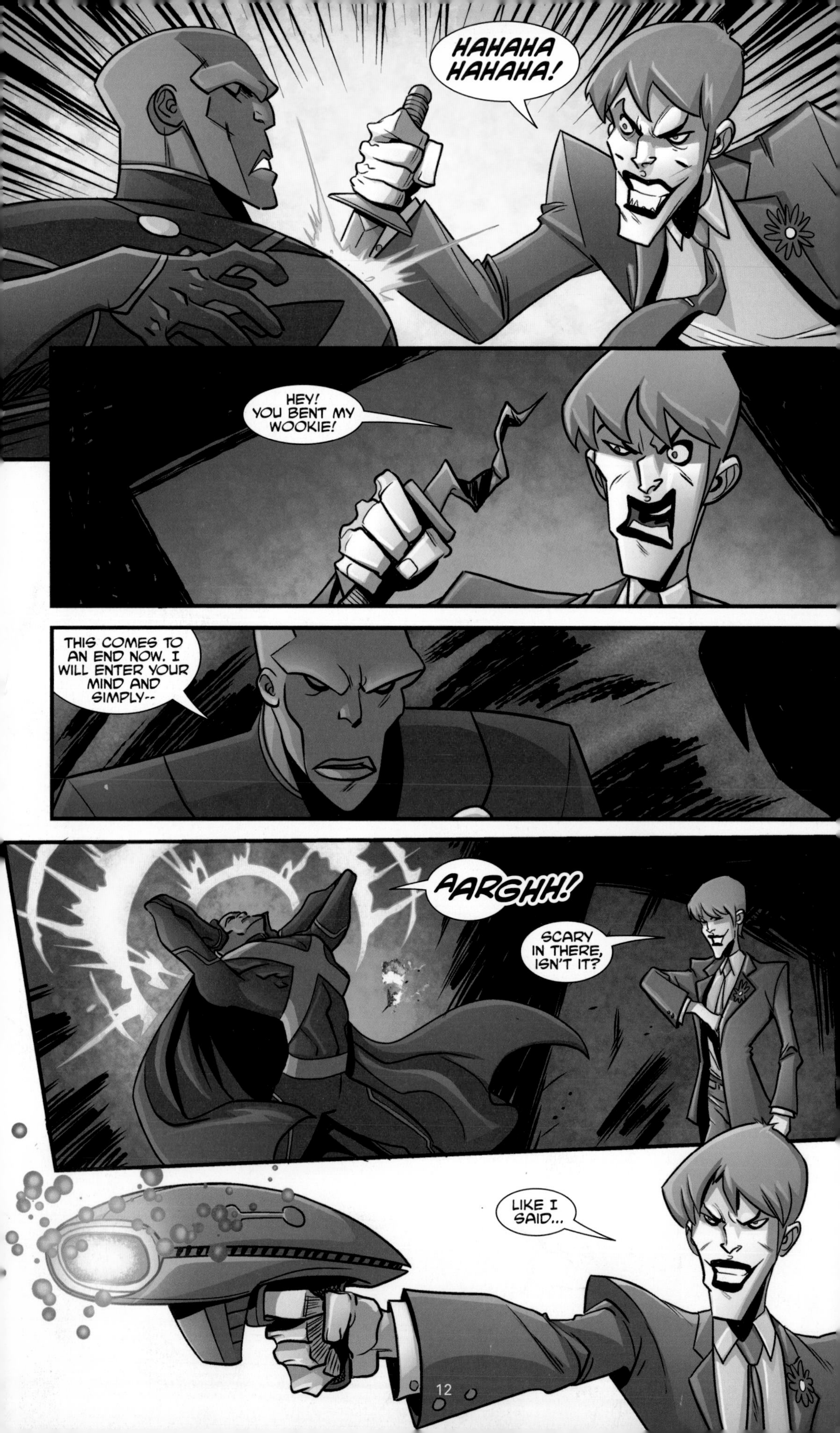
HAHAHA HAHAHA!
HEY! YOU BENT MY WOOKIE!
THIS COMES TO AN END NOW. I WILL ENTER YOUR MIND AND SIMPLY--
AARGHH!
SCARY IN THERE, ISN'T IT?
LIKE I SAID...

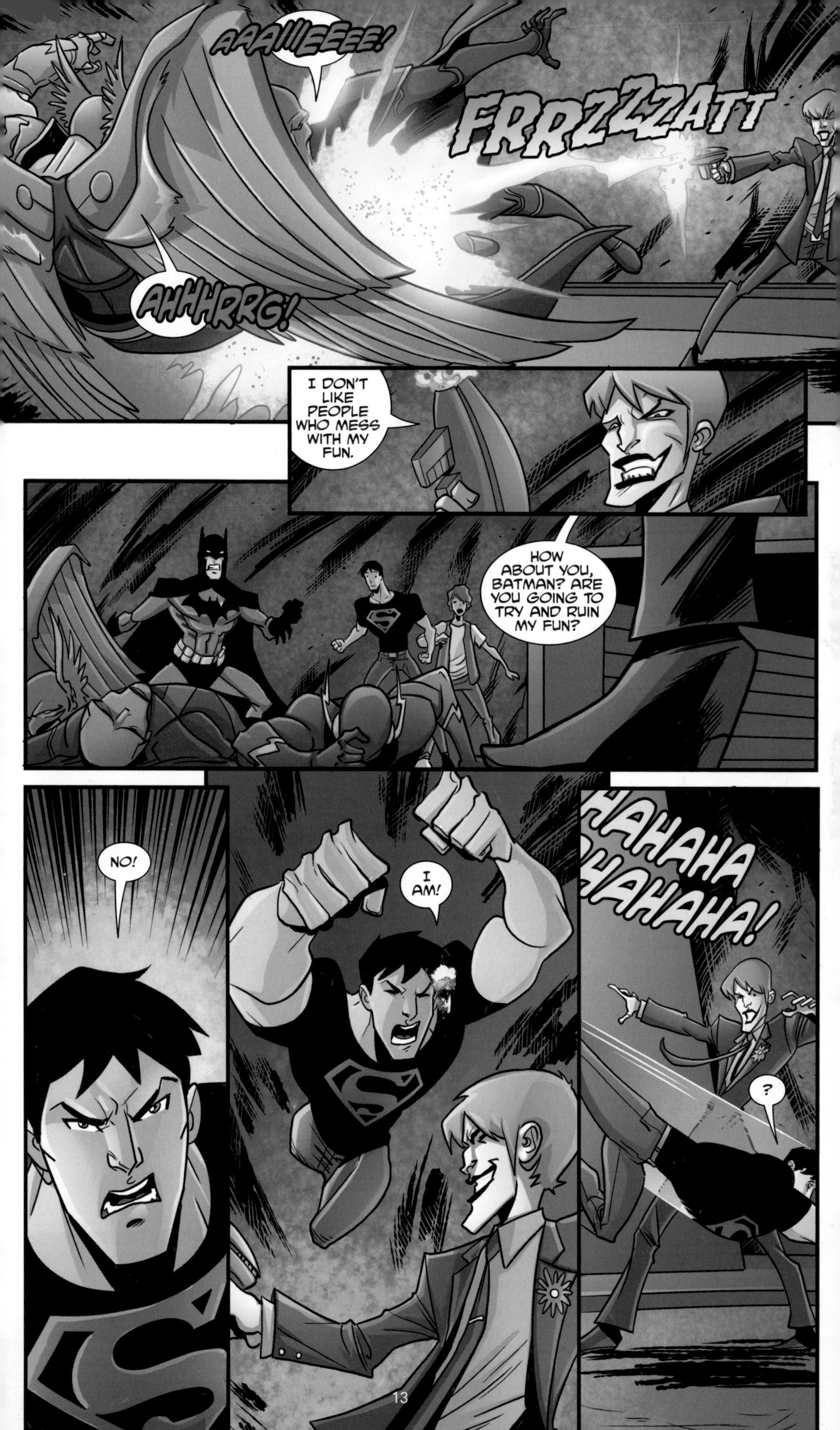
AAAIIIEEEEE!
FRRZZZZATT
AHHHRRG!
I DON'T LIKE PEOPLE WHO MESS WITH MY FUN.
HOW ABOUT YOU, BATMAN? ARE YOU GOING TO TRY AND RUIN MY FUN?
NO!
I AM!
HAHAHA HAHAHAHA!
?

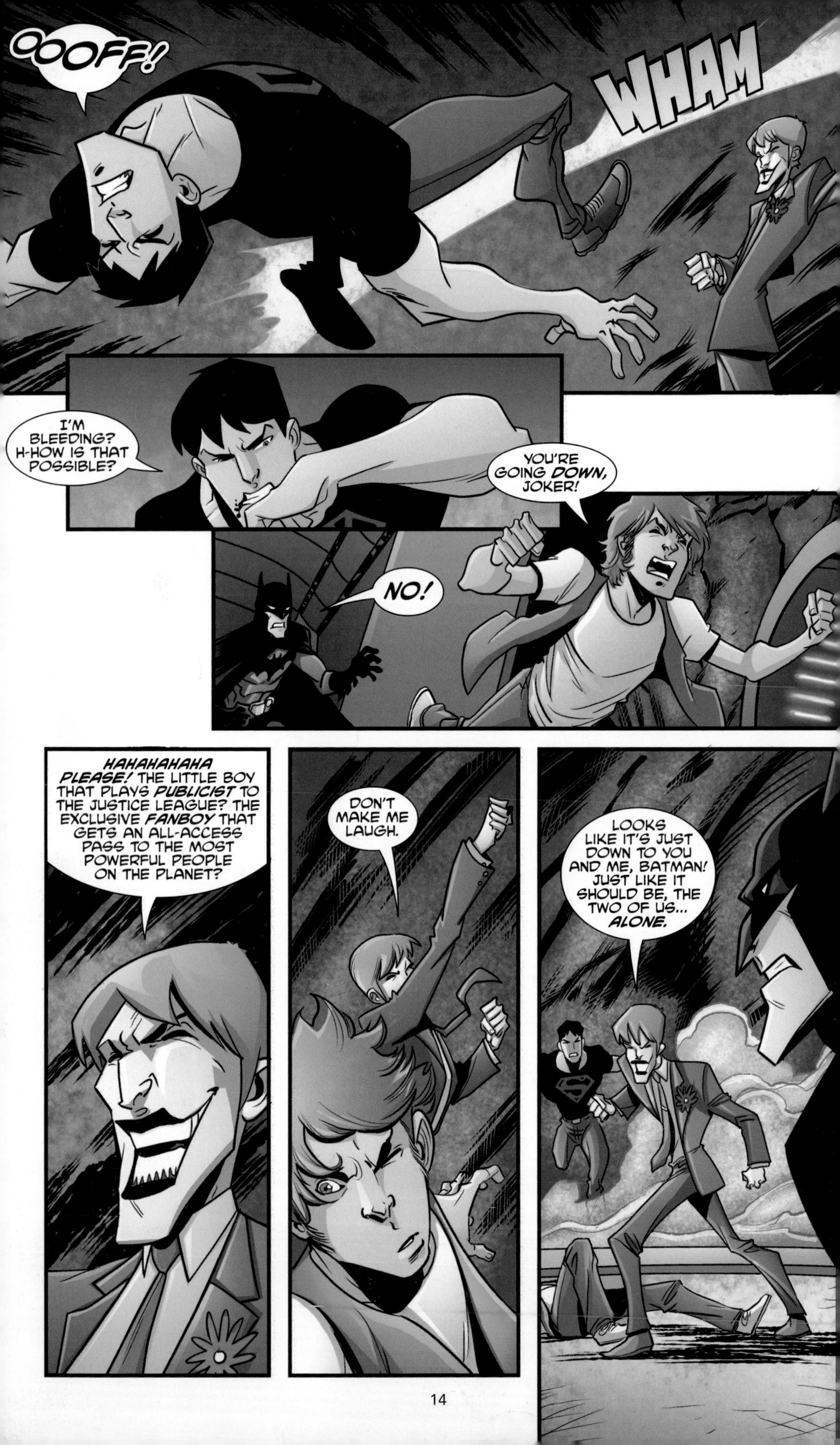
OOOFF!
WHAM
I'M BLEEDING? H-HOW IS THAT POSSIBLE?
YOU'RE GOING DOWN, JOKER!
NO!
HAHAHAHAHA PLEASE! THE LITTLE BOY THAT PLAYS PUBLICIST TO THE JUSTICE LEAGUE? THE EXCLUSIVE FANBOY THAT GETS AN ALL-ACCESS PASS TO THE MOST POWERFUL PEOPLE ON THE PLANET?
DON'T MAKE ME LAUGH.
LOOKS LIKE IT'S JUST DOWN TO YOU AND ME, BATMAN! JUST LIKE IT SHOULD BE, THE TWO OF US... ALONE.

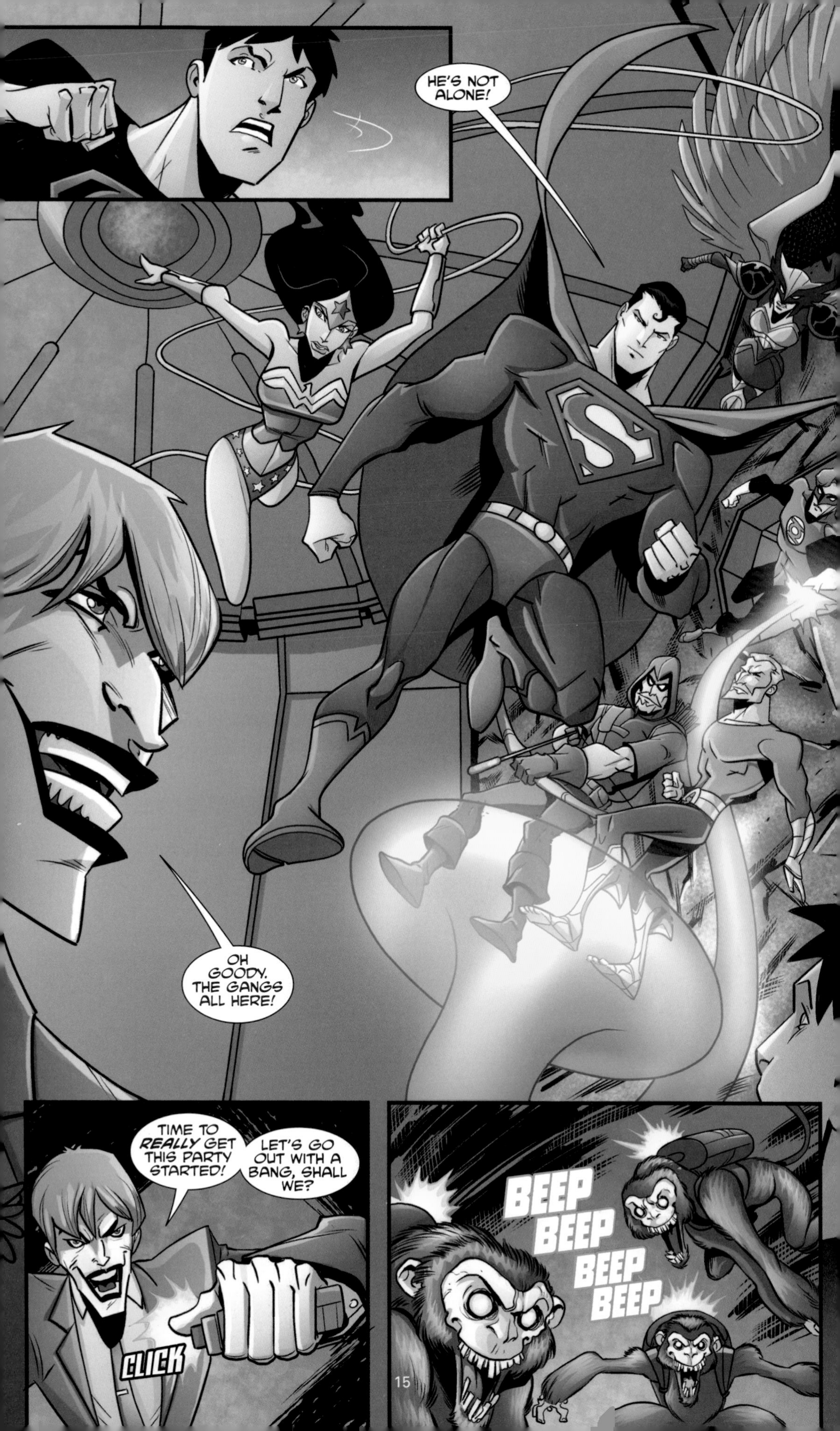
HE'S NOT ALONE!
OH GOODY. THE GANGS ALL HERE!
TIME TO *REALLY* GET THIS PARTY STARTED!
LET'S GO OUT WITH A BANG, SHALL WE?
CLICK
BEEP
BEEP
BEEP
BEEP

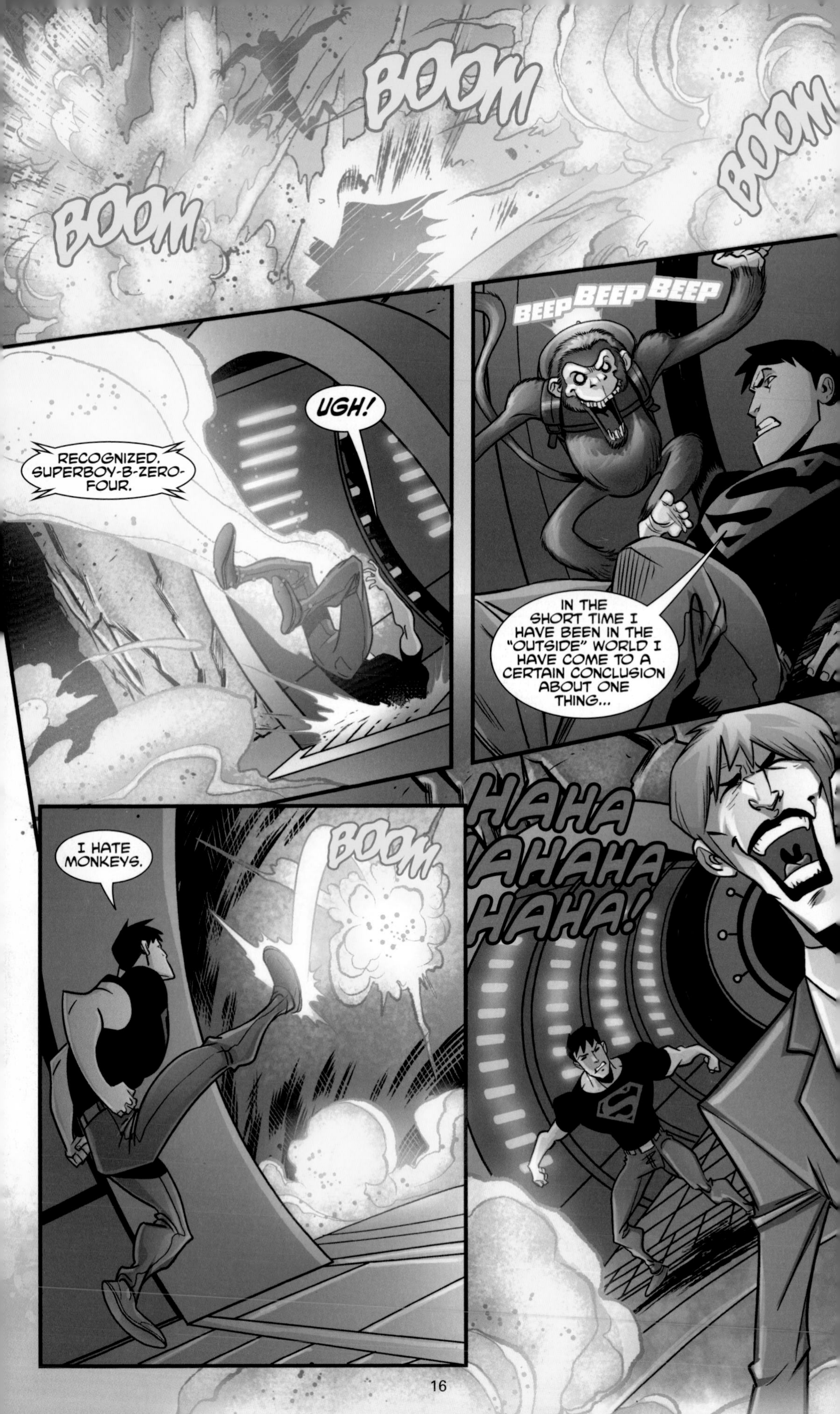
BOOM
BOOM
BOOM
UGH!
RECOGNIZED. SUPERBOY-B-ZERO-FOUR.
BEEP BEEP BEEP
IN THE SHORT TIME I HAVE BEEN IN THE "OUTSIDE" WORLD I HAVE COME TO A CERTAIN CONCLUSION ABOUT ONE THING...
I HATE MONKEYS.
BOOM
HAHA HAHAHA HAHA!

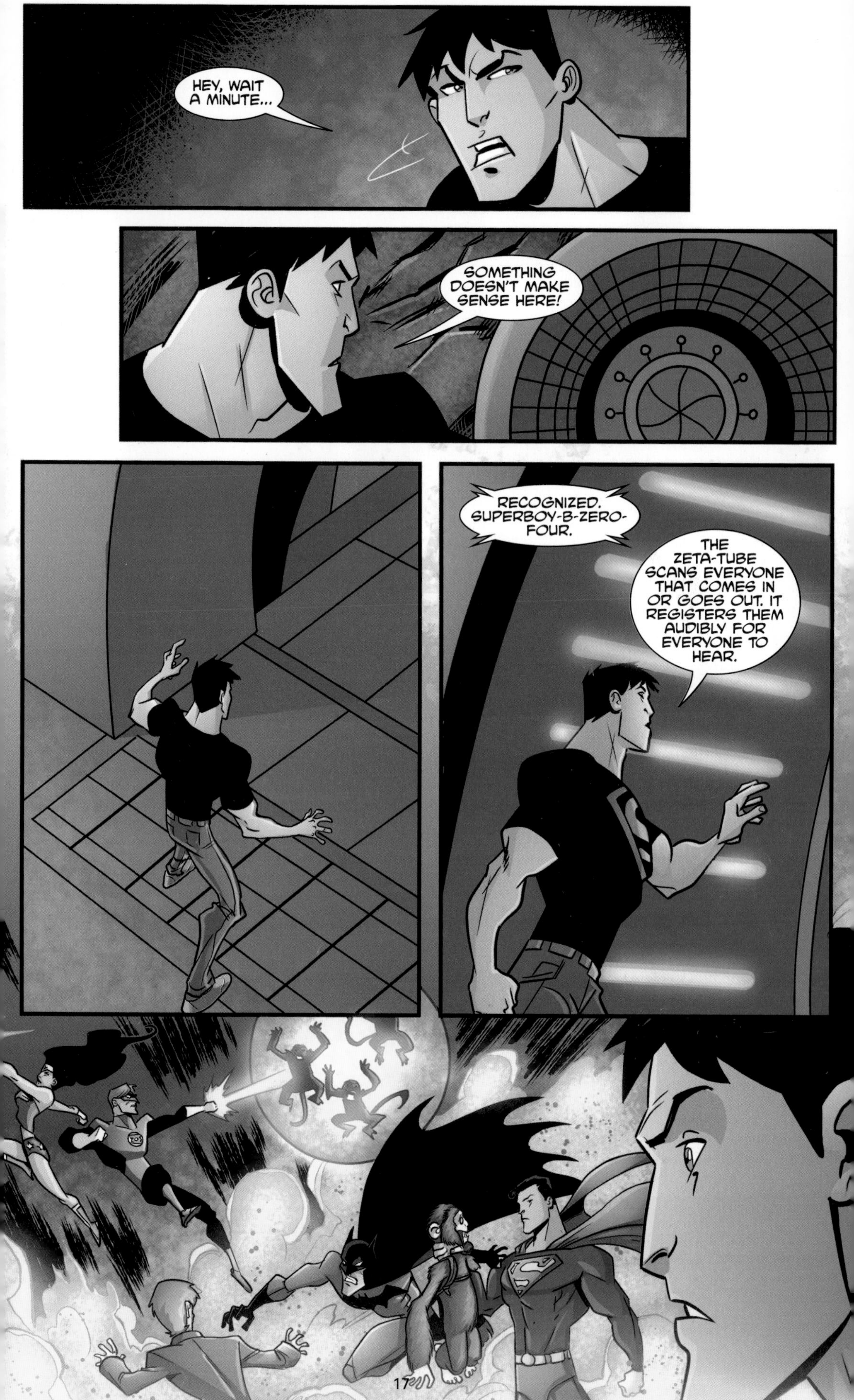
HEY, WAIT A MINUTE...
SOMETHING DOESN'T MAKE SENSE HERE!
RECOGNIZED. SUPERBOY-B-ZERO-FOUR.
THE ZETA-TUBE SCANS EVERYONE THAT COMES IN OR GOES OUT. IT REGISTERS THEM AUDIBLY FOR EVERYONE TO HEAR.

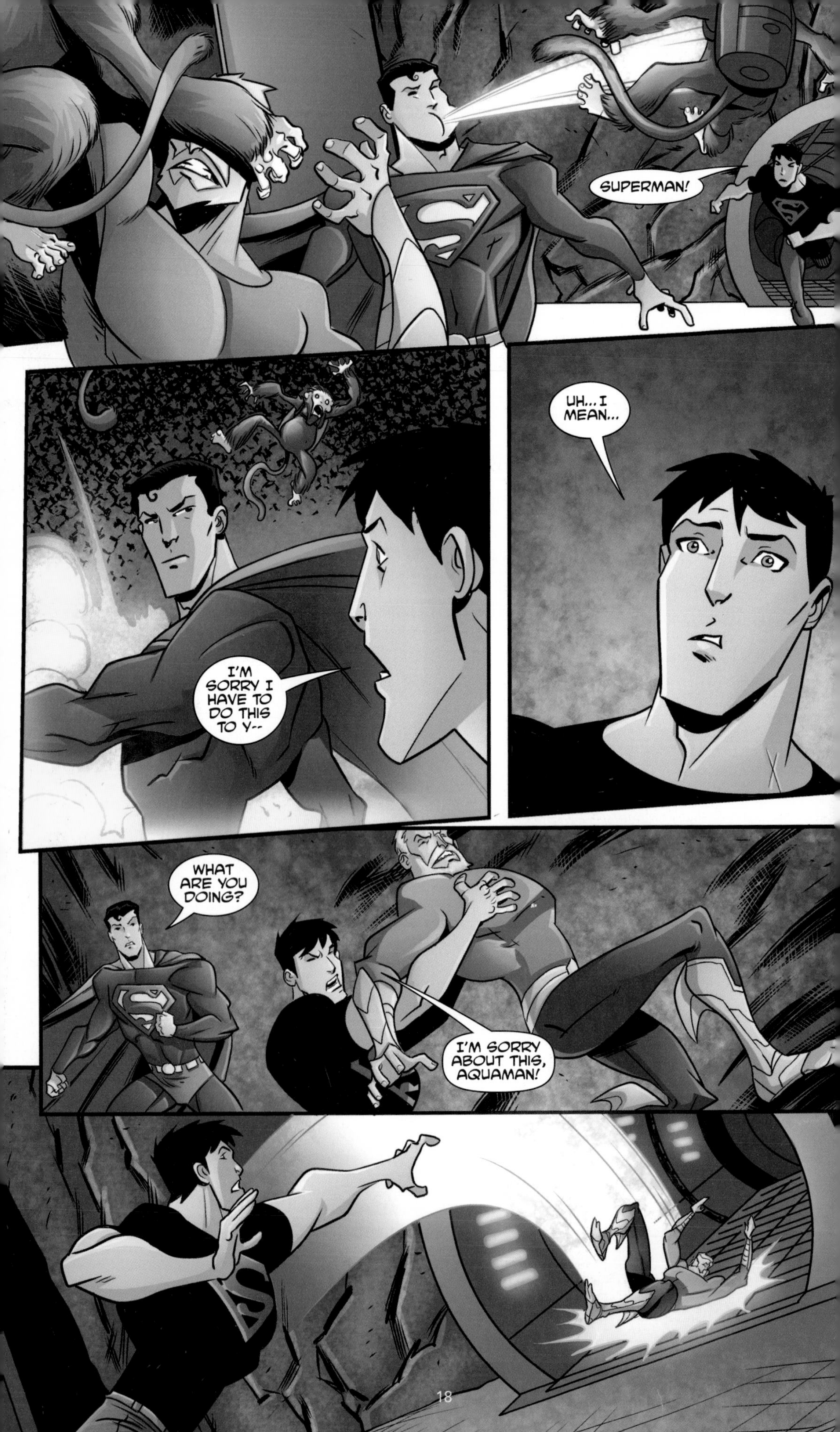
SUPERMAN!
I'M SORRY I HAVE TO DO THIS TO Y--
UH... I MEAN...
WHAT ARE YOU DOING?
I'M SORRY ABOUT THIS, AQUAMAN!

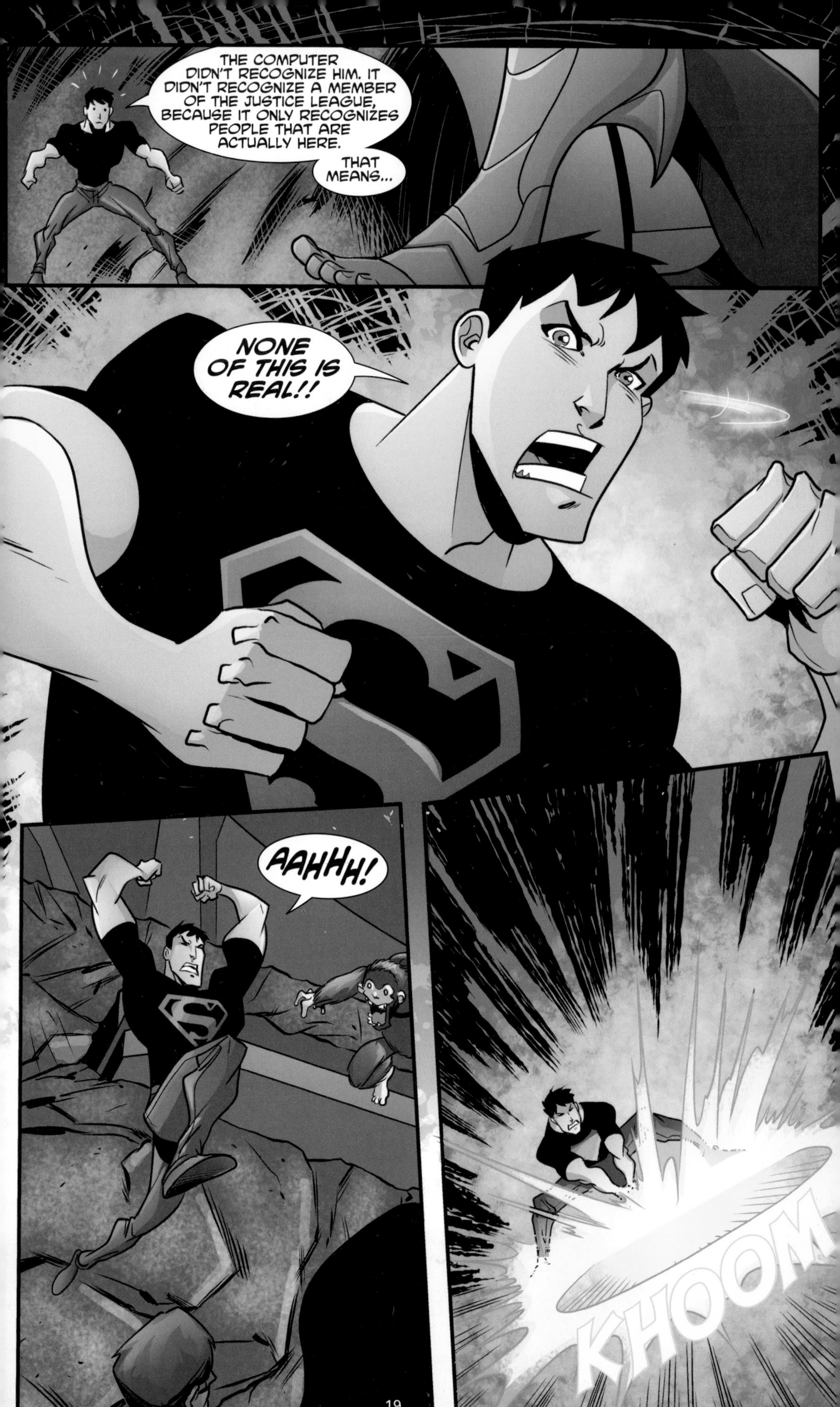
THE COMPUTER DIDN'T RECOGNIZE HIM. IT DIDN'T RECOGNIZE A MEMBER OF THE JUSTICE LEAGUE, BECAUSE IT ONLY RECOGNIZES PEOPLE THAT ARE ACTUALLY HERE.
THAT MEANS...
NONE OF THIS IS REAL!!
AAHHH!
KHOOM

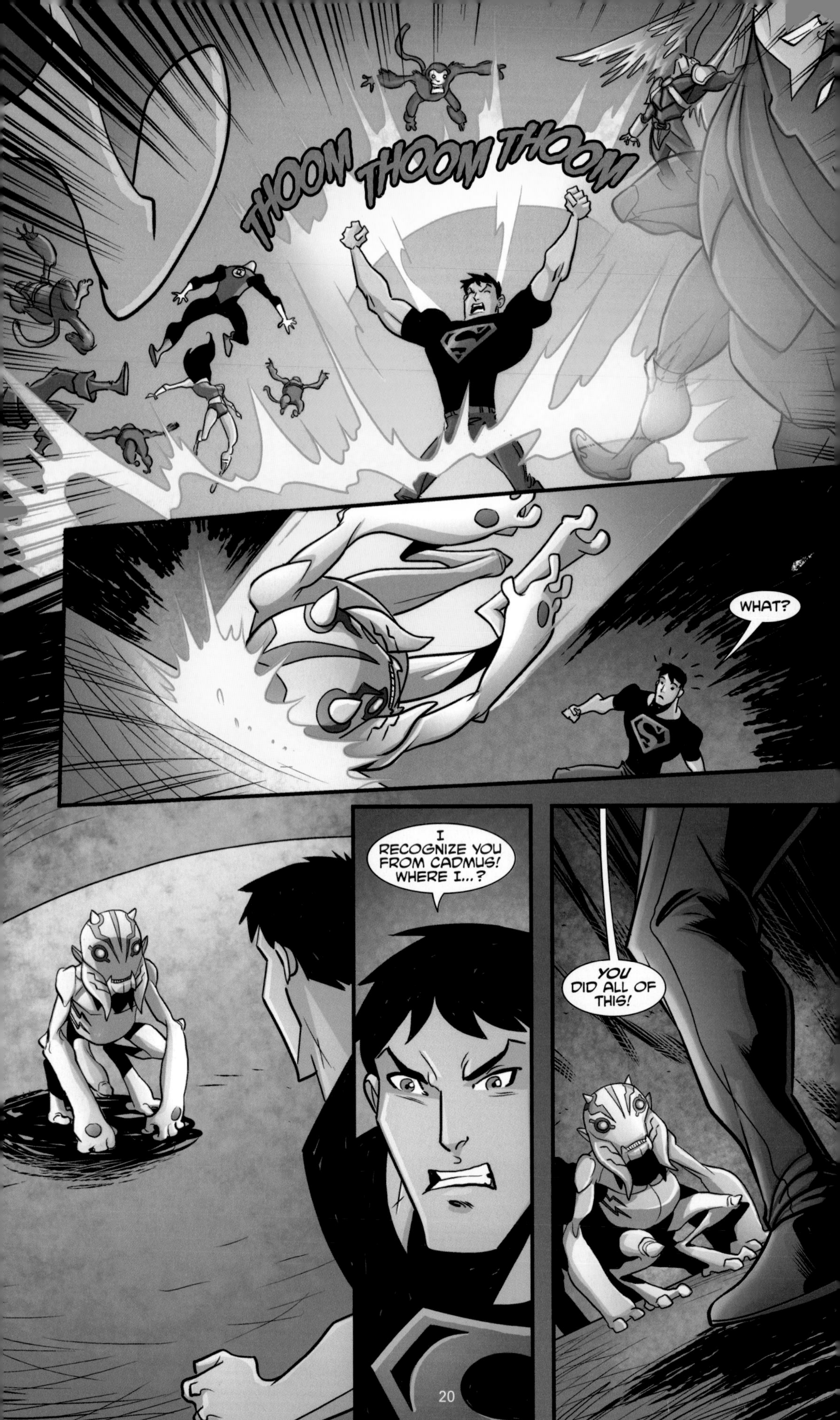
THOOM THOOM THOOM
WHAT?
I RECOGNIZE YOU FROM CADMUS! WHERE I...?
YOU DID ALL OF THIS!

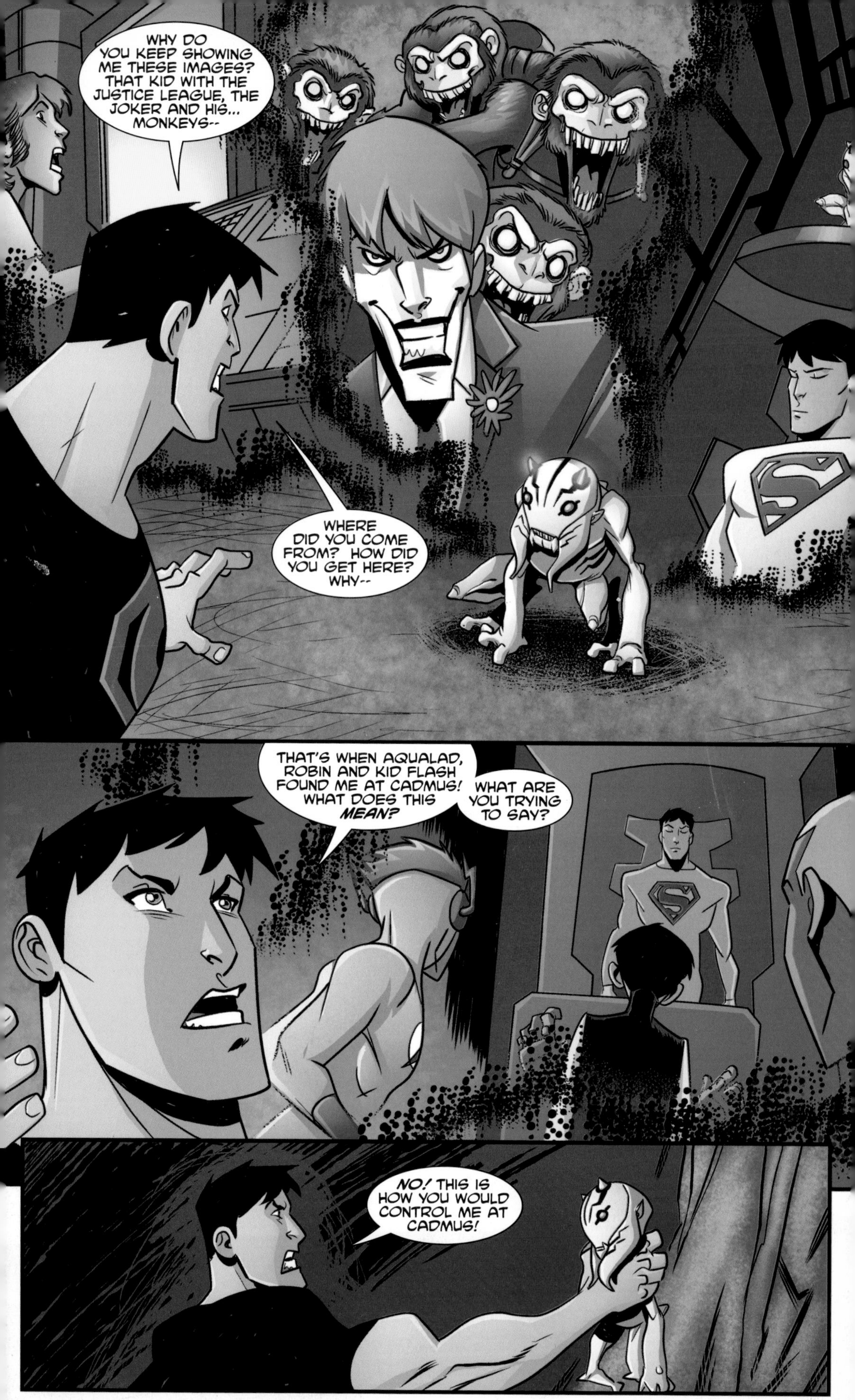
WHY DO YOU KEEP SHOWING ME THESE IMAGES? THAT KID WITH THE JUSTICE LEAGUE, THE JOKER AND HIS... MONKEYS--
WHERE DID YOU COME FROM? HOW DID YOU GET HERE? WHY--
THAT'S WHEN AQUALAD, ROBIN AND KID FLASH FOUND ME AT CADMUS! WHAT DOES THIS *MEAN?*
WHAT ARE YOU TRYING TO SAY?
NO! THIS IS HOW YOU WOULD CONTROL ME AT CADMUS!

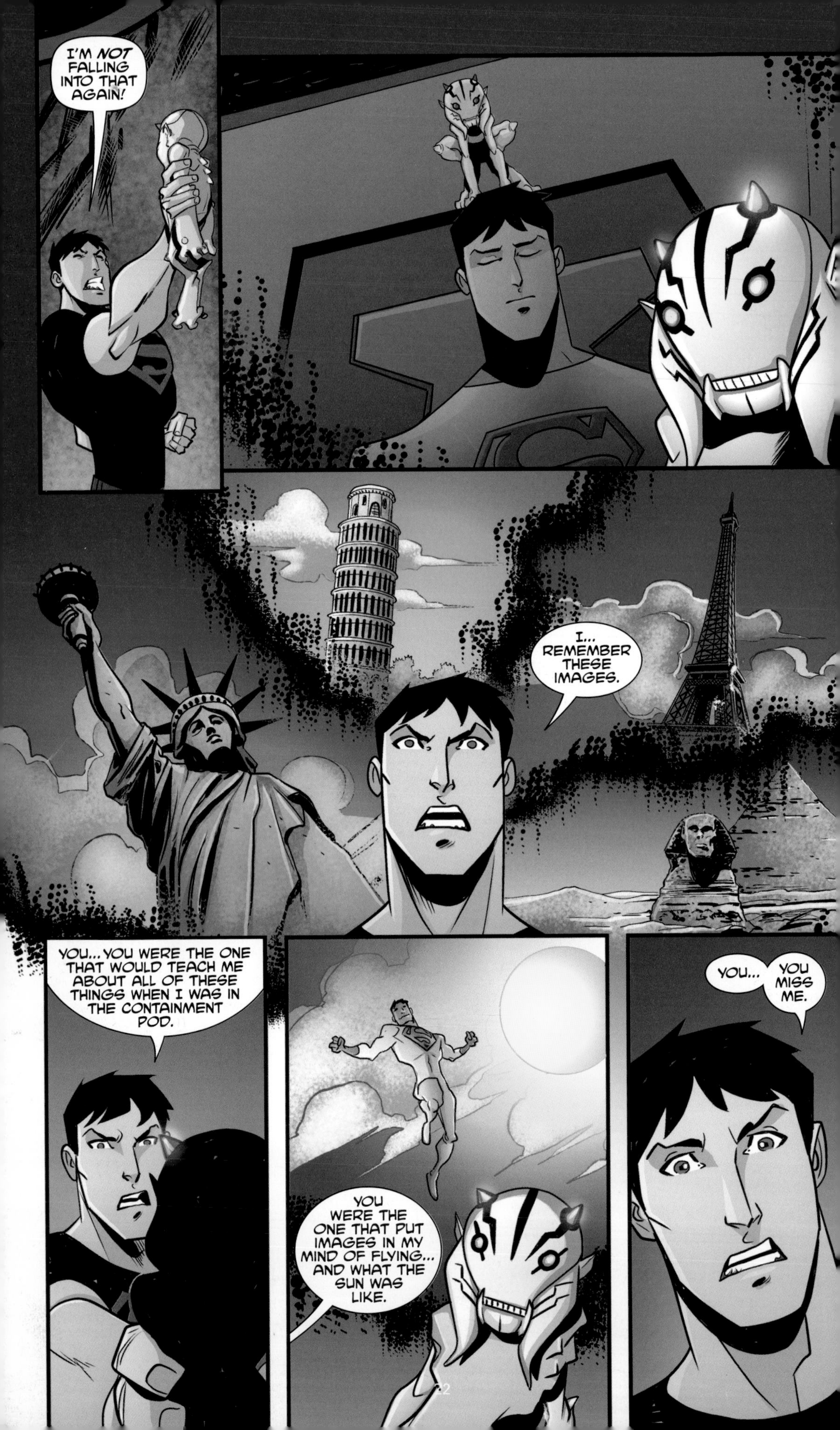
I'M *NOT* FALLING INTO THAT AGAIN!
I... REMEMBER THESE IMAGES.
YOU...YOU WERE THE ONE THAT WOULD TEACH ME ABOUT ALL OF THESE THINGS WHEN I WAS IN THE CONTAINMENT POD.
YOU WERE THE ONE THAT PUT IMAGES IN MY MIND OF FLYING... AND WHAT THE SUN WAS LIKE.
YOU...
YOU MISS ME.

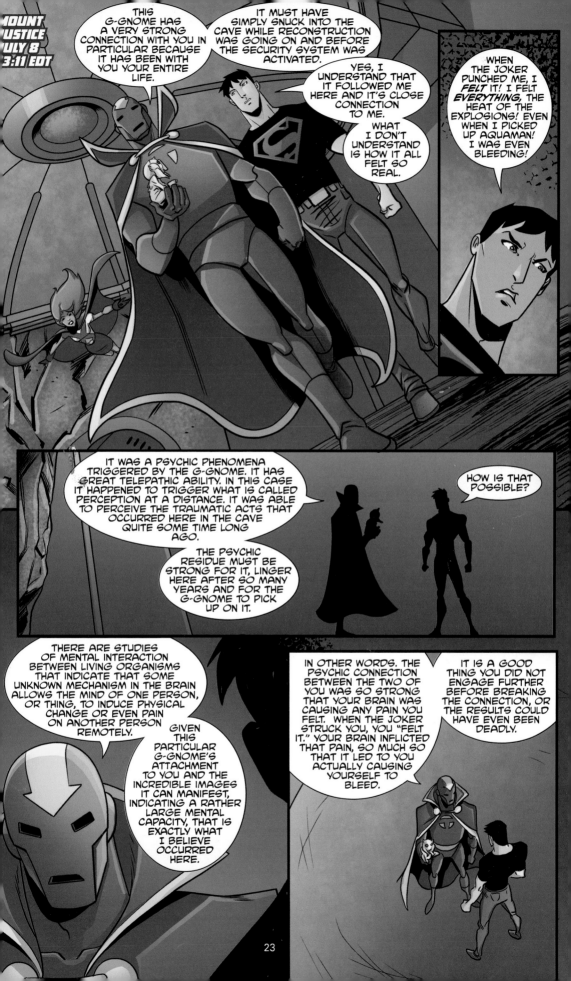

THIS G-GNOME HAS A VERY STRONG CONNECTION WITH YOU IN PARTICULAR BECAUSE IT HAS BEEN WITH YOU YOUR ENTIRE LIFE.

IT MUST HAVE SIMPLY SNUCK INTO THE CAVE WHILE RECONSTRUCTION WAS GOING ON AND BEFORE THE SECURITY SYSTEM WAS ACTIVATED.

YES, I UNDERSTAND THAT IT FOLLOWED ME HERE AND IT'S CLOSE CONNECTION TO ME.

WHAT I DON'T UNDERSTAND IS HOW IT ALL FELT SO REAL.

WHEN THE JOKER PUNCHED ME, I *FELT* IT! I FELT *EVERYTHING*, THE HEAT OF THE EXPLOSIONS! EVEN WHEN I PICKED UP AQUAMAN! I WAS EVEN BLEEDING!

IT WAS A PSYCHIC PHENOMENA TRIGGERED BY THE G-GNOME. IT HAS GREAT TELEPATHIC ABILITY. IN THIS CASE IT HAPPENED TO TRIGGER WHAT IS CALLED PERCEPTION AT A DISTANCE. IT WAS ABLE TO PERCEIVE THE TRAUMATIC ACTS THAT OCCURRED HERE IN THE CAVE QUITE SOME TIME LONG AGO.

THE PSYCHIC RESIDUE MUST BE STRONG FOR IT, LINGER HERE AFTER SO MANY YEARS AND FOR THE G-GNOME TO PICK UP ON IT.

HOW IS THAT POSSIBLE?

THERE ARE STUDIES OF MENTAL INTERACTION BETWEEN LIVING ORGANISMS THAT INDICATE THAT SOME UNKNOWN MECHANISM IN THE BRAIN ALLOWS THE MIND OF ONE PERSON, OR THING, TO INDUCE PHYSICAL CHANGE OR EVEN PAIN ON ANOTHER PERSON REMOTELY.

GIVEN THIS PARTICULAR G-GNOME'S ATTACHMENT TO YOU AND THE INCREDIBLE IMAGES IT CAN MANIFEST, INDICATING A RATHER LARGE MENTAL CAPACITY, THAT IS EXACTLY WHAT I BELIEVE OCCURRED HERE.

IN OTHER WORDS. THE PSYCHIC CONNECTION BETWEEN THE TWO OF YOU WAS SO STRONG THAT YOUR BRAIN WAS CAUSING ANY PAIN YOU FELT. WHEN THE JOKER STRUCK YOU, YOU "FELT IT." YOUR BRAIN INFLICTED THAT PAIN, SO MUCH SO THAT IT LED TO YOU ACTUALLY CAUSING YOURSELF TO BLEED.

IT IS A GOOD THING YOU DID NOT ENGAGE FURTHER BEFORE BREAKING THE CONNECTION, OR THE RESULTS COULD HAVE EVEN BEEN DEADLY.

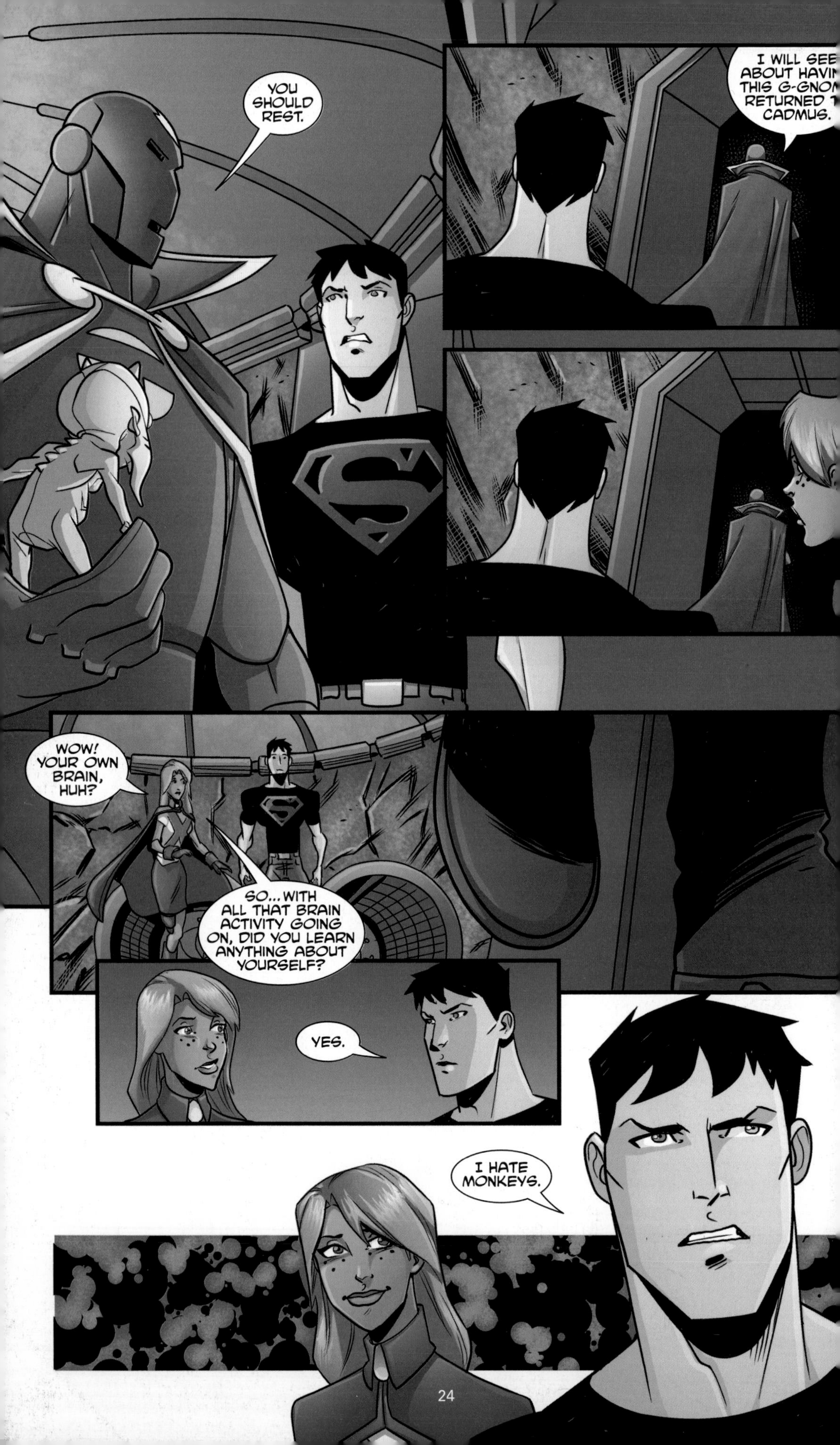
YOU SHOULD REST.
I WILL SEE ABOUT HAVIN THIS G-GNOM RETURNED T CADMUS.
WOW! YOUR OWN BRAIN, HUH?
SO... WITH ALL THAT BRAIN ACTIVITY GOING ON, DID YOU LEARN ANYTHING ABOUT YOURSELF?
YES.
I HATE MONKEYS.

WILL TROUBLE FIND YOUNG JUSTICE AGAIN...?

Read the next action-packed adventure to find out!

DC COMICS
YOUNG JUSTICE
HACK AND YOU SHALL FIND
BALTAZAR · FRANCO · NORTON

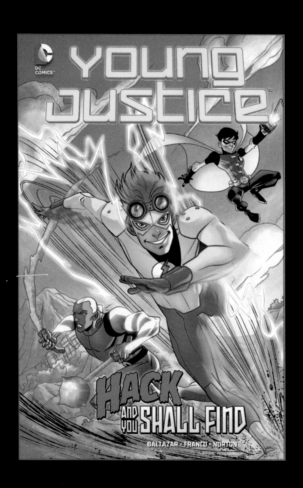

CREATORS

ART BALTAZAR WRITER

Art Baltazar is a cartoonist machine from the heart of Chicago! He defines cartoons and comics not only as an art style, but as a way of life. Currently, Art is the creative force behind *The New York Times* best-selling, Eisner Award-winning, DC Comics series Tiny Titans, and the co-writer for Billy Batson and the Magic of SHAZAM! and co-creator of Superman Family Adventures. Art is living the dream! He draws comics and never has to leave the house. He lives with his lovely wife, Rose, big boy Sonny, little boy Gordon, and little girl Audrey. Right on!

FRANCO AURELIANI WRITER

Bronx, New York born writer and artist Franco Aureliani has been drawing comics since he could hold a crayon. Currently residing in upstate New York with his wife, Ivette, and son, Nicolas, Franco spends most of his days in a Batcave-like studio where he produces DC's Tiny Titans comics. In 1995, Franco founded Blindwolf Studios, an independent art studio where he and fellow creators can create children's comics. Franco is the creator, artist, and writer of Weirdsville, L'il Creeps, and Eagle All Star, as well as the co-creator and writer of Patrick the Wolf Boy. When he's not writing and drawing, Franco also teaches high school art.

MIKE NORTON ARTIST

Mike Norton has been a professional comic book artist for more than ten years. His best-known works for DC Comics include the series Young Justice, All-New Atom, and Green Arrow/Black Canary.

GLOSSARY

engage (en-GAYJ)--busy doing something, or occupied doing something

fanboy (FAN-boi)--a fanboy, or fangirl, is someone who is extremely interested or obsessed in a specific thing, like comics

lapse (LAPS)--a small mistake or failure, or the passing of time

maniac (MAY-nee-ak)--someone who is insane or acts in a wild or violent manner

manifest (MAN-uh-fest)--if you make something manifest, you make it appear or you create it

metabolism (muh-TAB-uh-liz-uhm)--the process by which our bodies change the fuel we eat into the energy we use to breathe, digest, and carry on all other important life functions

phenomena (fuh-NOM-uh-nah)--very unusual, remarkable, or miraculous

publicist (PUHB-luh-sist)--a person who promotes or markets a company or group's message or purpose

threat (THRET)--a person or thing regarded as a danger

toxin (TOK-sin)--a certain type of poison

vigilance (VIJ-uh-luhnss)--being watchful and alert, or committed to something

VISUAL QUESTIONS & PROMPTS

1. This panel is seen from a certain point of view. Whose eye do you think we're seeing the action through? Why do you think the artists chose to illustrate the panel in this way?

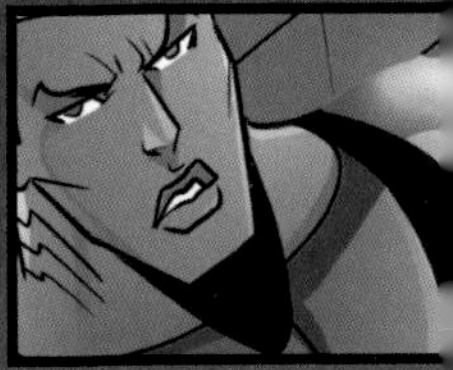

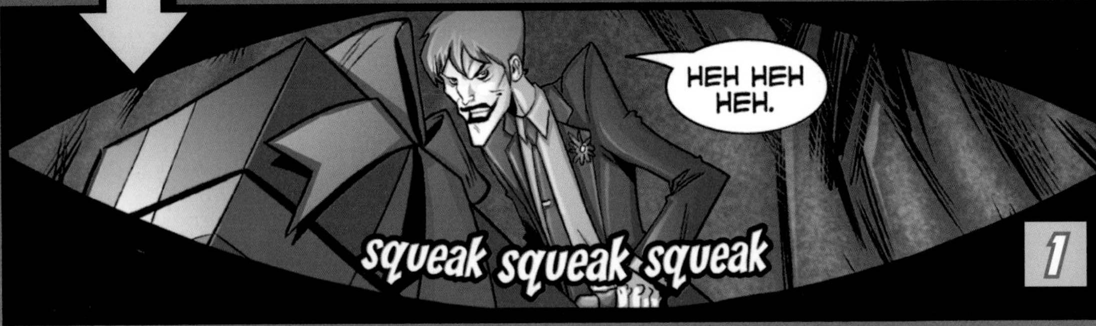
HEH HEH HEH.
squeak squeak squeak
1

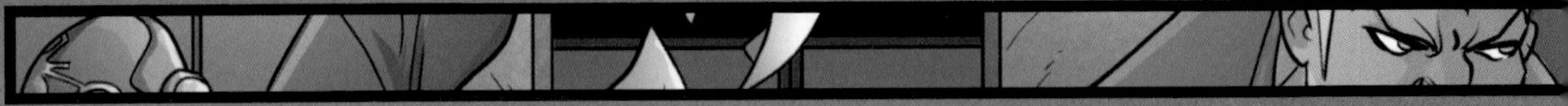

2. The members of the Justice League use their respective powers to help each other and work together. Explain how Hawkman, the Flash, and Martian Manhunter use their abilities to help each other in the panel below.

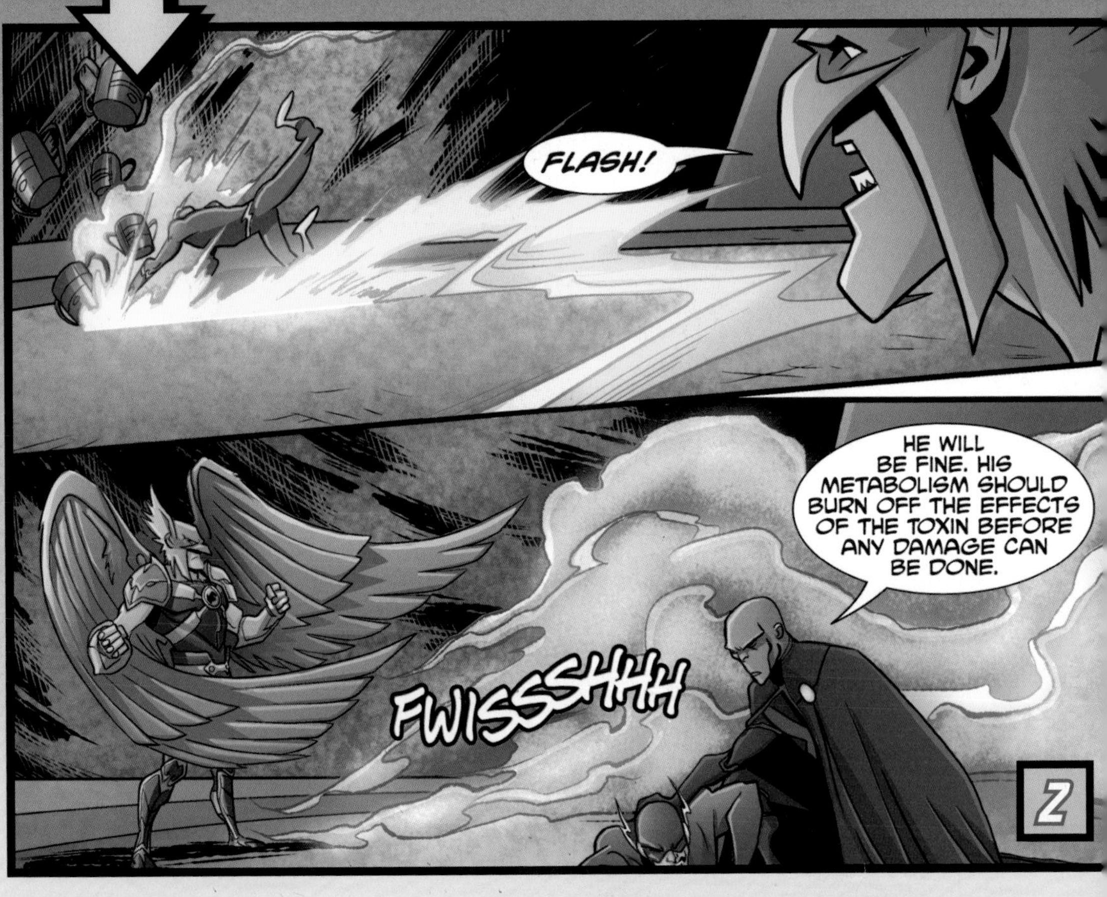
FLASH!
HE WILL BE FINE. HIS METABOLISM SHOULD BURN OFF THE EFFECTS OF THE TOXIN BEFORE ANY DAMAGE CAN BE DONE.
FWISSSHHH
2

3. What do you think the lines around Martian Manhunter's head mean? Why? How do they make you feel?

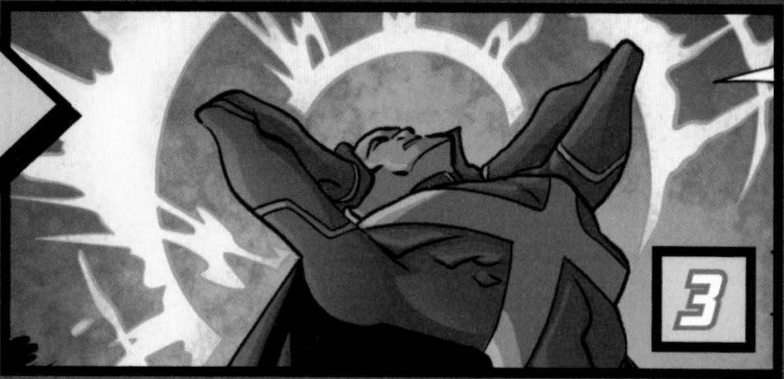
3

4. The panel below is something called a montage, or a combination of several different images. How does the dialogue in the word balloons relate to the text? Do you think the art matches the words well? Why or why not?

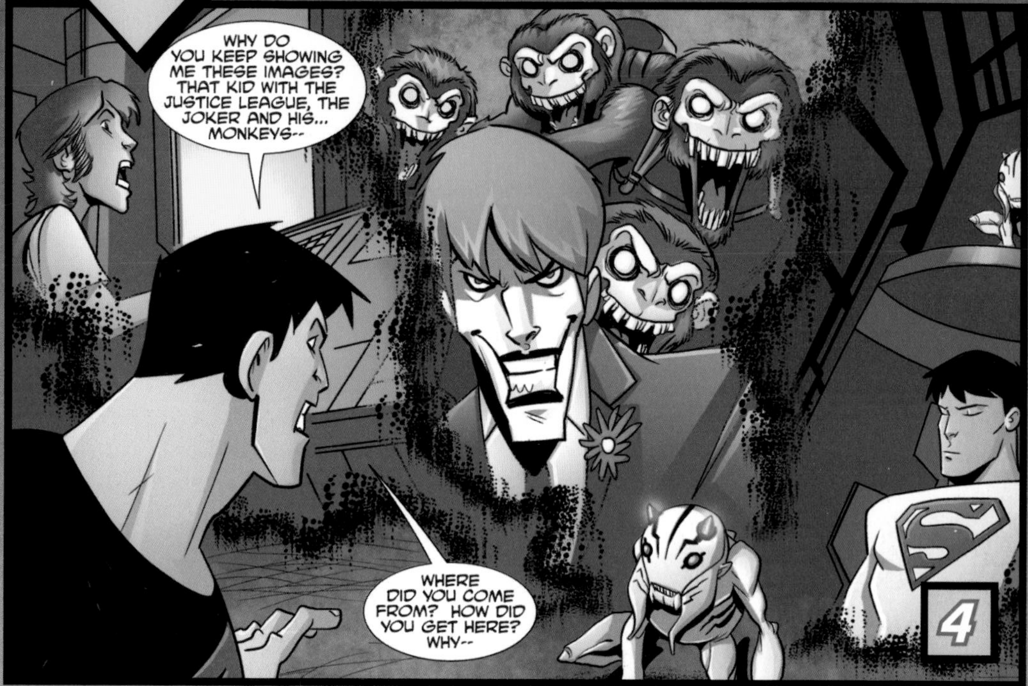
WHY DO YOU KEEP SHOWING ME THESE IMAGES? THAT KID WITH THE JUSTICE LEAGUE, THE JOKER AND HIS... MONKEYS--
WHERE DID YOU COME FROM? HOW DID YOU GET HERE? WHY--
4

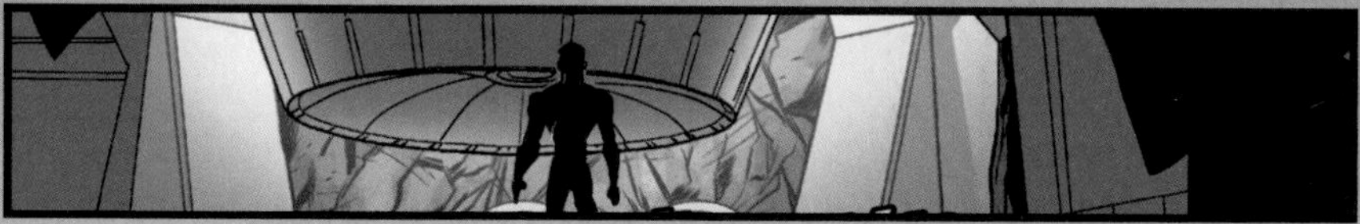

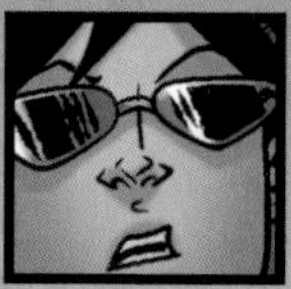

5. What do you think this G-Gnome's posture means? Is he scared? Ready to attack? Why?

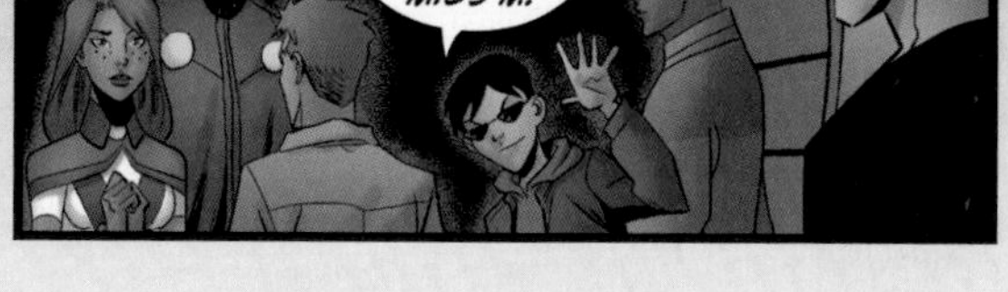
HEY, SUPERBOY! COME MEET *MISS M.*

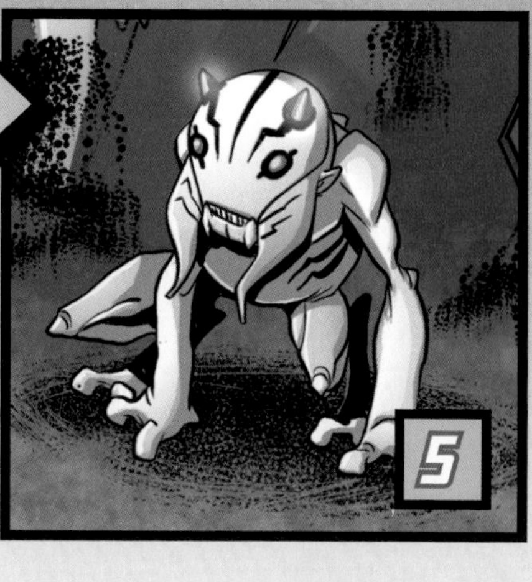
5

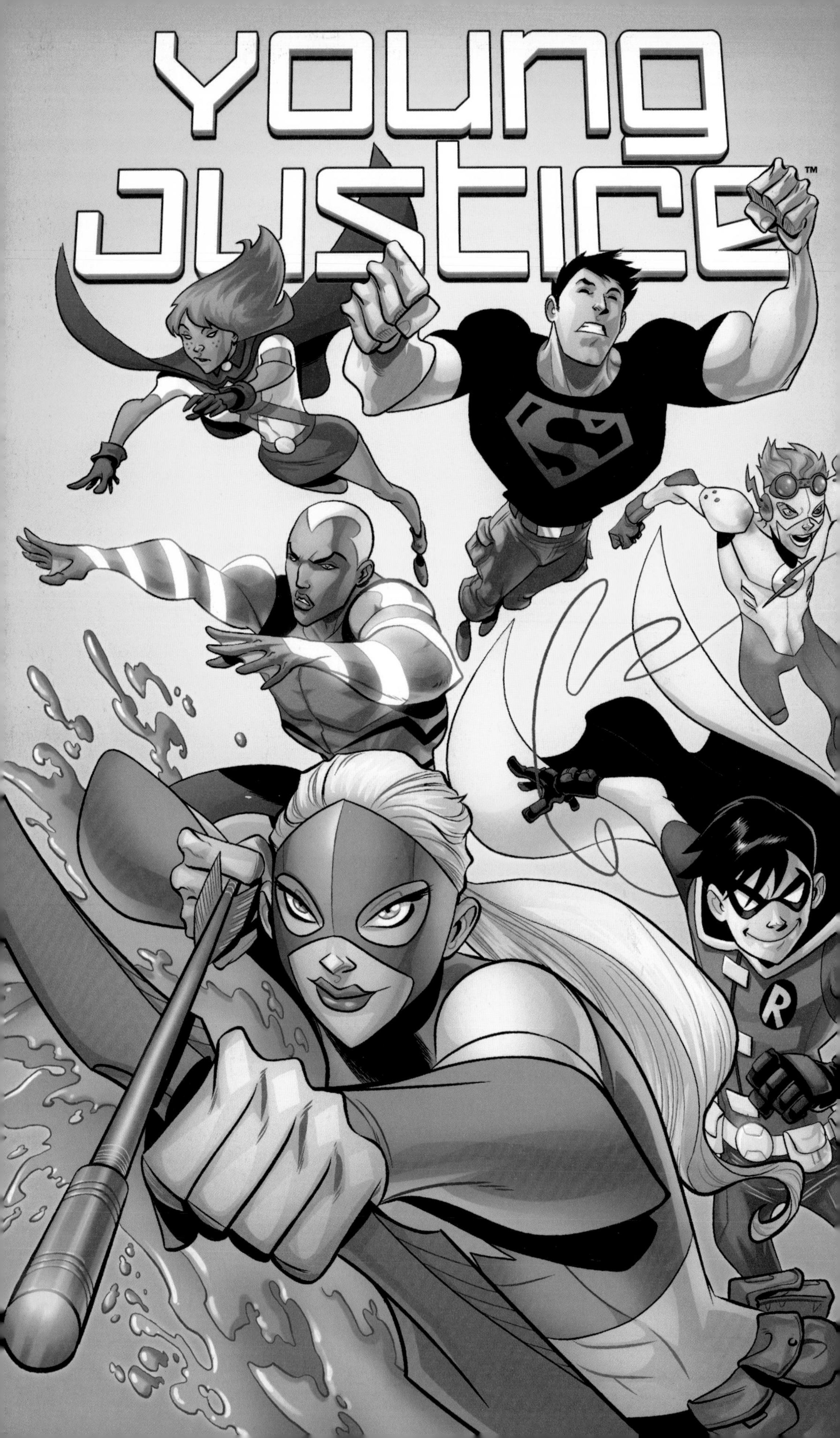
YOUNG JUSTICE™

READ THEM ALL!

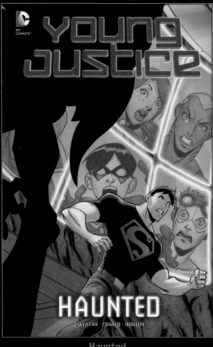

Haunted

Monkey Business

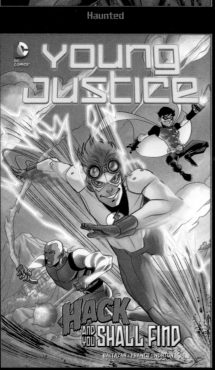

Hack and You Shall Find

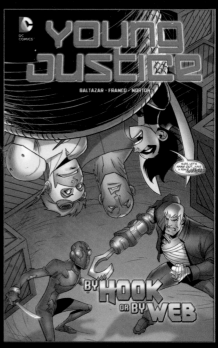

By Hook or By Web

only from...

young justice ™